DESIRED

TWO MARKS - 3

VANESSA VALE
RENEE ROSE

WANT FREE RENEE ROSE BOOKS?

In addition to the free stories, you will also get bonus epilogues, special pricing, exclusive previews and news of new releases.

GET A FREE VANESSA VALE BOOK!

Join Vanessa's mailing list to be the first to know of new releases, free books, special prices and other author giveaways.

http://freeromanceread.com

PROLOGUE

ACHEL

CHESTER, my so-called boyfriend, pulled up in front of my parents' Palo Alto mansion and parked his convertible BMW in the circle drive. From the window, I couldn't miss the pale blue shirt, or the way his dark hair was perfect. That meant he had more product in it than I ever used in mine so it wasn't wind tousled. He was perfect at all times. *Perfect.*

Ugh. I'd been dodging him for three days. *He's perfect for you, darling. Think of it, you'll be a senator's wife someday! It'll be perfect when you're married to a man with such aspirations. Your children will be perfect.*

Perfect. *Perfect.* PERFECT. My parents didn't understand that I didn't want perfect. That I wanted to choose my own man, one with flaws. Was it too much to ask to own my own life? To do my own thing? Make my own choices? Fail, even?

Failing didn't happen in my family. It was considered impossible in the political spotlight my family lived in.

I'd graduated from Stanford, like my father and grandfather before me. I was smart, and didn't need coddling. Or being told what to do. Like marriage. To Chester. The wedding I hadn't planned. The one that was being thrust upon me by Chester and my parents.

I just needed a minute to breathe and figure out what I really wanted to do instead of becoming Mrs. Chester Barnes IV. The *perfect* wife.

I'd made it crystal clear to them, I didn't want to get married. I didn't want Chester. I'd been hinting for years at a life that didn't involve my parents' closest friends' son. To become arm candy as Chester worked his way up in my father's law firm and into politics. He needed me and my family's clout to win.

Since I was going to become a senator's wife, I wanted more of a life than vote stumping, planning charity events, and wearing fashionable dresses. Glancing down at myself, I took in the blue dress, the navy pumps. Pearls. God, my mother must have told Chester what I was going to wear so we matched.

Matched!

My heart galloped in my chest with anxiety and panic. No matter what I said, my life was being planned for me. Everyone was ready for me to step into the mold they'd created for me. To continue the family legacy. It wasn't as if they ever considered *me* to be the senator.

Chester let himself in the house without knocking since my parents already thought of him as their son-in-law. "Rach? Babe?" he called. "Come on, we're going to be late."

I sighed and left my childhood bedroom before he came up and invaded my space any more. The only good thing was that my parents insisted we wait until marriage before living together. I'd added on that I was saving myself for marriage. I remembered that night, when I'd told Chester of that. It made me smile even now.

For once, he hadn't gotten his way. It wasn't that he was overly gentlemanly, but because he didn't want to blow any chances with my father. The future lawmaker was willing to take some cold showers.

But for not much longer.

"Late for what?" I asked. "I thought you were taking me to dinner."

"I am. I made reservations." He had already started up the stairs as I sailed down them, pausing to receive a perfunctory kiss. I felt nothing from it. Where was the heat? The pulsing between my legs I read about in my romance novels? Why was the perfect hero seemingly *too* perfect?

"Well, I don't think they'll give our table away if we're two minutes late," I said.

He followed me back down the steps and across the foyer. "Are you ready? You look ready."

My stomach twisted. I really needed to break things off with him. To just end it. Say I didn't want him. That we weren't a 'thing.' That he should find someone else who'd be happy to wear matching outfits and be eager for early tee times. Nothing about us worked for me, and I was getting tired of pretending it did.

Tonight. I'd do it at dinner tonight, where we were in public and he couldn't make a scene.

"Sure. I'm ready." I needed to get this over with.

I struggled to think of something to say as we cut through the ritzy neighborhood, but it didn't matter, because Chester launched into a ten-minute long boast about his latest racquetball sessions, only taking a breath when he pulled in front of the valet at the country club.

I looked around. "Wait. We're having dinner here?" I'd grown up coming to this place. It wasn't romantic or private. Not a place I wanted to go on a date.

"Uh, yes." He came around and joined me by the entrance. "I figured for old time's sake. We practically grew up here together, right?"

I'd grown up coming to the club. But together? Hardly. Chester was five years older, so most of our childhood had been him leading his group of friends to pick on mine. But okay, whatever.

I also didn't understand why he'd need reservations. It wasn't like the restaurant was ever over-full. It was a private club, and both our families were members.

"Come on, we're through here," Chester said, taking my hand and leading me around to a side entrance that led to one of the private dining rooms.

My pulse started to pick up, and not in a good way.

Crap. Chester had something planned.

And here I thought the surprise would be me breaking up with him.

But it had to be done.

He opened the door and put a hand on my back to usher me in.

"Surprise!"

A loud chorus of voices shouted at once, making me jump and scream.

The lights flipped on, and I blinked.

A large banner was strung across the far wall. *Happy Engagement Chester and Rachel.* No comma after *engagement,* which for some reason was the first thing I noticed. Not the actual words.

Because the actual words were... untrue. We weren't engaged. He hadn't asked. I definitely wouldn't have said yes.

"Wh... what's this?" My high-pitched voice sounded more like my mother's than my own.

My parents, and Chester's, and a bunch of random family friends all stood around the large table with broad smiles. There were presents in the middle like it was already our wedding night. Not that we were having a wedding night.

"It's a surprise engagement party," my mother explained, coming over and hugging me. Her familiar scent swirled around me, cloyingly sweet and heavy. "Isn't it wonderful, dear?"

I tried to take a step back, but Chester's hand at my back stopped me. "Um... but we're not engaged," I managed to say.

Chester pulled out a box, and dropped to one knee.

There were a few gasps, but all I saw was the box. The ring. It was big and gaudy. Something easily picked up in photos.

Oh no. Oh, crap. My stomach dropped. Panic made it feel like the walls were closing in.

"Chester, no." I tried to stop him.

He looked up at me with an adoring, eager expression. "Rachel, will you do me the honor of becoming my wife?"

I shook my head. I'd gone along with everyone for so long, but I couldn't do it now. Not here, not like this. This wasn't what I wanted. Maybe I'd enabled everyone by not saying *no* before, but now I was.

"No. No way."

I was able to back up, and I did. One step, then another.

Quickly.

I backed right up until I hit the closed door, then I reached behind my back and twisted the handle.

"This... um... I can't... this is not, um..."

Torn between being the good girl who didn't want to embarrass Chester, and my fury at him and my family for banking on that good girl saying yes for exactly that reason, I opted out of any explanation at all.

"I won't marry you."

I turned and ran, as fast as I could. From the life they had planned for me. The life I didn't want.

1

 ORD

HUNGER WAS what took me to the diner for lunch. As usual, I'd lost track of time—between patients and my research, it was a common occurrence—and arrived well past the busy lunch rush. For such a small town, it was good to see all the business in West Springs. Locals—humans and shifters—took care of their own. As I settled into my usual booth in the corner, I breathed in the scents. Chili. Chicken pot pie. Vegetable soup. Fall had set in, the leaves past their peak and the trees were almost bare once again, which meant warm and comforting foods on the menu.

I hadn't been in for a while, having been away for over a week at a medical conference in Texas, then tackling back-to-back patients to make up for lost time.

Something was different today. I took a deep breath and tried to figure it out. A new spice? Fruit pie? I noted hints of cinnamon and cherry. Perhaps Bessie had found a new recipe. My mouth watered, eager to try it. I was a confirmed bachelor in town, so Bessie ensured I ate well. Being the only doctor in West Springs, I kept the humans in town healthy, which kept me busy all hours of the day and night. Then there was my research into shifter DNA and gene mapping that distracted me.

Like now. I missed the blur of a woman as she pushed through the swinging doors into the kitchen, followed by a clatter and breaking of dishes as they hit the floor. I winced and hoped only empty plates had been dropped instead of food that would be wasted.

A minute later, Bessie came out, wiping her hands on a dishtowel. Seeing me in the corner, she offered me the usual smile and wave, then veered to the coffee pot. She came over with a mug and filled it to the brim.

"How's it going today?" she asked.

While she couldn't ask me after my patients

because of confidentiality, she knew as much, if not more, about the residents of West Springs than I did. I might know who had bursitis—humans—or how fast someone healed after a fall on a full moon run—shifter—but she knew everything else.

"You tell me," I replied.

She set her free hand on her hip and took a deep breath. At sixty, she was as spry as ever. Her two mates kept her busy. One was in the kitchen cooking, the other on their ranch on the back side of the mountain, keeping everything running.

"Sally's eager for her baby to be born." She looked left and right to see who was sitting nearby. She didn't dare say *pup* in the restaurant because of all the humans. "I'm sure you know that."

I didn't need to treat any of the shifters, since they healed on their own from all but the most severe of injuries, like beheading or being shot with a silver bullet. Both of which were possible, but I'd never known it to happen. I did follow the reproduction of our species closely.

"Little Jack Morring's cow won a blue ribbon at the fall fair last weekend. Still no grumblings from the ranchers. Well, no more than usual," she went on.

I frowned and took a sip of my coffee. I loved it black and strong, and Bessie knew just how to make it to strip paint off a barn. Over the summer, two ranchers had killed some wolves, and been given fines for their actions. Since they had been the ringleaders of the group of older and pestering humans, the remaining group who frequented the diner for their morning coffee klatch didn't have the same drive to put action to their anger. Thankfully.

"That's good to hear." I took a sniff, picking up that delicious dessert scent. "Got a new pie you're trying out?"

She frowned. "Pete made a batch of his potato soup."

The scent definitely wasn't that.

A woman came in from the kitchen with a tray on her shoulder but it leaned dangerously toward spilling. She was the one I'd glimpsed before, but could now watch. I could check out her curvy body, the way the diner uniform t-shirt clung to her full breasts. The way her blonde hair slid like a curtain over her shoulders.

My mouth watered, eager to brush that hair to the side and kiss her neck. To nip at the spot where it met her shoulder.

Going to a table of men on the other side of the diner, she began to serve them. She had a difficult time balancing the tray, and I was practically on the edge of my seat with the need to rescue her. All of the meals had safely been placed on the table, but a glass of iced tea spilled, pouring off the edge of the tray like a dark waterfall.

Her instant reaction was to turn away from the diners, which flung the liquid across the tile floor.

The sweet scent was stronger now, and I couldn't tear my gaze away from the woman. A flush of pink brightened her cheeks, clearly from embarrassment. She set the tray on an empty table and bent down to wipe up the spilled drink with a cloth she'd had tucked into the apron at her waist. Her jeans were snug across her curvy ass, and I couldn't look away.

Neither could the men at the table. I saw red, and a growl escaped my throat.

Bessie held out a hand. "If I told off every man who looked at one of my waitresses with a little extra attention, there'd only be female customers." I didn't like her words and glared at her, but only for a second because I had to look back at *her*. Because I'd been just like those men, ogling her. Hell, my dick was hard just watching her from across the room.

"Who is that?" I had to know. It wasn't just important, it was imperative. I couldn't leave here without that information, and anything else Bessie had on her.

All I knew was that she was around twenty, gorgeous...
and mine.

Wait, what?

"Rachel."

Rachel.

"She's new. As you can tell. She's as smart as a tack,
figuring out the checks without using a calculator."
Bessie leaned down, although she wasn't whispering
for me. She did it so Rachel couldn't overhear, which
meant she was human. "The worst waitress I think I've
ever had. She's broken more dishes than she's served,
but on the bright side, my floor's never been cleaner
with all the wiping up."

Then she laughed, to soften the harsh words.
She'd been in the business for decades, so it was
saying a lot. I took offense for Rachel.

"If she's so terrible, why did you hire her?" I asked.

Pete hollered from the back for Bessie. She
huffed, then turned on her sneakered foot, not
answering.

I wanted to go and yell at her mate for interrupting
what I could learn about Rachel, but then I'd come
across as insane.

Which I felt at this moment.

What was wrong with me? I itched to stand and
toss Rachel over my shoulder. Carry her off. Help her

with her tables. Put her coat on her before she left so she didn't get cold.

"Rach, hon, help the doc with his order while I see what Grumbly Pants in the back wants," Bessie said.

Rachel stood from her crouch and nodded to Bessie, then glanced my way.

Holy shit. Her eyes were the palest of blues. Intense. Frustrated and upset. She raised a finger to me, then went and poured a new glass of iced tea and took it to the waiting table. Then she came my way.

Finally.

I took her in up close. Fuck, she was young. Her skin was flawless. Her eyes were bright, and her smile a little forced. "Hi there. I'm Rachel. What can I get for you today?"

She nodded and her hair swung around her cheek. I wanted to reach out and tuck it back. Wrap it around my fingers and hold it as I kissed her. Taking a deep breath, I tried to calm my raging heart... and dick.

Then it hit me. This was the sweet scent I'd picked up. Her.

She was the dessert I craved. She was the cherry pie, and I knew why. I sounded like a horny asshole, but I knew just by looking at her that she was sweet. And the reason I scented cherries was because she had one. Fuck me. My dick spurted pre-cum, and my wolf, who was usually quiet and tame, surged forward and licked his lips. She was a virgin. It wasn't as if she had a sign on her forehead, but I knew. I'd bet my medical license on it. Crazy, yeah.

She. Was. My. Mate.

"I, uh, I'll have some more water," I choked out.

Unaware of my porn-worthy thoughts, she nodded and headed to the kitchen.

I barely remained in my seat, but remembered at the last second that following her with a raging hard-on wouldn't be smart. I was the town doctor. I was always in control. It was my job to have a level head. To be calm and collected. A quick thinker.

Now, I was out of control. Wild. Driven by my basest needs to make her mine.

I'd never expected to meet my true mate. To find the scent of her. Because, while I'd been born in West Springs and was a pure-bred member of the Two Marks pack, I had no scent match. Meaning there wasn't another male whose scent was the same as mine. Who would claim a mate with me. The quirk of the West Springs shifter DNA. Hell, I knew all about it, since I studied it with a passion.

I was the broken one. The kind I studied the most. Yet, while I'd now found my mate, I couldn't claim her as a Two Marks mate should. I was alone, and I was deficient. Not only did I not have a scent match, but I couldn't give her or the pack the pups that were deserved. And our species was rapidly dwindling.

Rachel returned with a glass of ice water. She kept her eyes on mine the whole way over, as if she sensed something different about me too. As if she were attracted. Needy.

Her nipples poked against the t-shirt, giving her away. I took a deep breath. Her scent was even sweeter now. Fuck, she was aroused. I scented her desire. Her need.

For me. This wasn't one-sided.

No. I'd be hers as much as she'd be mine.

She closed the distance between us, but at the last second, she stumbled. The ice water flew over me, the freezing liquid drenching me. The glass dropped to the floor and broke.

"Oh my God, I'm so sorry!" Rachel cried.

I'd never been thankful for being doused in ice water before. My dick went down. Until she pulled a rag from her apron pocket—she must have grabbed a new one after the iced tea incident—and started drying my chest and then the front of my pants.

Now I was so hard, I was sure the zipper would break. Her hands froze and she looked up at me, meeting my gaze. Her eyes were so blue, like a summer sky. In those depths, I saw her. Recognized her. Knew she was mine.

I had no idea how long we stared, but she blinked, yanked her hand back from my jean-covered dick, then turned away. Her cheeks flushed a bright pink, and it was obvious she was mortified. She squatted down and began to pick up the broken glass.

"No, don't get that," I warned. "You'll—"

She hissed, then sucked her finger into her mouth. Shit, she'd cut herself. Before I could reach out and see how badly she was hurt, she popped up and ran for the kitchen, the swinging door moving back and forth from her haste.

I stared after her, stunned.

Her scent lingered, and my wolf howled. I'd found her, and now she was gone. I stood and followed. I'd dwelled on all the reasons why I shouldn't keep a mate, but now that I knew who she was, all I could think about was being with her. I couldn't let even a room separate us.

Not now. Not ever again.

2

ACHEL

I BOLTED for the kitchen and went to the utility closet for a broom and dustpan. No, to escape, and pray the earth would split open and swallow me.

Dear Lord, I was the world's worst waitress. Hands down. There had to be an award for it. One would think a lifetime of eating out would have prepared me to wait on other people, but no. God, no. I was horrible.

Why hadn't Bessie fired me yet?

I didn't forget people's orders—that was the one thing I could do right. I could tally up meal totals without a calculator. But I was clumsy. I couldn't seem to balance all the dishes on the tray. I hadn't worked a shift yet where I didn't break a dish. Or spill something on someone.

But this was the worst. Had I seriously just rubbed that guy's water-soaked crotch with a towel?

It could probably be construed as sexual assault considering the... reaction I'd caused. I wasn't going to forget the thick bulge in the hot guy's jeans.

I leaned a shoulder against the wall beside the utility closet, stared down at the small cut on my finger, and tried to catch my breath. My heart was beating so frantically, I thought I might have a heart attack.

"Hey, are you okay?" A deep voice rumbled from behind me. It was *him*.

Oh God—he followed me! The kitchen seemed to swoop around me. Something about this guy made me feel breathless and hot and dizzy all at once.

"You cut yourself, and I wanted to check on it."

I spun around, my face still hot from our last encounter a few moments ago. "I am *so* sorry," I sputtered, not meeting his eyes. "And really embarrassed."

He came closer. My pulse raced. My skin tingled everywhere. I'd never had this reaction to a man before. I'd only dated Chester, although it wasn't like we ever went to dinner and a movie. Or bowling. A little laugh escaped me when I thought of Chester wearing loaner shoes.

It had been a given that he was my boyfriend ever since our mothers had said so when I turned sixteen, and he had graduated from college. But I'd known I was supposed to marry him for longer than that. It had been *Chester and Rachel* pretty much since birth.

The guy stepped right into my space, and took my wrist to examine my cut finger. It was only a little scratch, but it did sting, right along with my pride. A jolt of electricity ran up my arm at his touch. My nipples chafed against my bra.

Now that he wasn't sitting, his true size was obvious. If we were outside, he'd block the sun. I came up to his chin, and those shoulders... wow. Broad and sturdy. *All* of him was sturdy. Powerful and strong. Yet his touch was gentle.

"Cord's a doctor, honey," Bessie said from the doorway. "Let him have a look at that cut."

"Oh, um, it's nothing," I said, although blood dripped from the nick in my middle finger.

Of course he was a doctor. There wasn't any other reason for him to chase after me. Just because I had tingles—in all kinds of places—from his touch didn't mean he felt them in return.

"I'm sorr—" I broke off as our gazes locked and the breath left my chest.

I stared. He stared. My cut was forgotten. Even the fact that I had a finger.

I'd recognized how handsome he was the minute he walked into the diner, but now, up close, I found him devastating. Delicious. A square jaw, and smile lines around his green eyes, which had an amber glow to them.

His nostrils flared like he was drinking in my scent, and I had the strangest urge to do the same with him.

"As Bessie said, my name's Cord and I am a doctor. Don't be sorry or embarrassed." His voice was an earthy rumble that seemed to belong only to me. "Let's stop this bleeding." He guided me toward the waitress station where the napkins were neatly stacked, and grabbed one from the top of the pile.

He wrapped it around my finger and held it, but instead of looking at my wound, he continued staring into my eyes.

"I haven't seen you in the diner before," he murmured.

He was only holding my finger and we stood in the middle of the diner's kitchen, but nothing had ever felt so intimate. It was like only the two of us existed and we were long lost lovers. I didn't look away to see if Bessie remained.

"I-I just started. A few weeks ago. I'm a terrible waitress. Clumsy." I couldn't take my eyes off him. This might have been the definition of mesmerized.

"You're perfect," he corrected, and my mouth fell open. "I'd like to get some antiseptic on this cut. Let me take you to my clinic. It's just around the corner."

"Oh, I couldn't..." I finally managed to tear my gaze from him to glance at Bessie, who still hovered nearby, her hands on her hips, taking in this crazy scene.

Bessie didn't look at me. She was staring at Cord, with what seemed to be surprise. Then a slow smile spread across her face. "Cord?"

"Yes," he replied, not looking away from me. The one word was deep and final.

"Well butter my butt and call me a biscuit," she replied, then laughed.

I frowned at her, because it seemed they'd just had a full conversation, and I had no clue what I'd missed.

"Go on with him, Rachel," Bessie told me, watching Cord with avid interest. "I can't have you bleeding all over the diner. Your shift's almost over, anyway."

"Oh, um, are you sure?" I asked. I had hurt myself on the job. I wasn't going to sue her or anything after my clumsiness, but it happened. I didn't want to do anything—else—to jeopardize my job, so if she wanted me to have the cut tended to...

"I'm sure, let our doctor bandage you up," she replied, nodding her head. "He looks like he won't rest until you do."

Cord was already guiding me past the swinging doors and into the main dining area. "She's right. I'll always take care of you."

Oh.

"Hang on, let me grab my purse," I said, grateful for the few brain cells that seemed to still be working.

Cord seemed reluctant to release my hand, but he did, and I grabbed my hot pink Kate Spade purse from beneath the counter.

We walked out of the diner together as I held the napkin around my finger. He took my other hand in his. It seemed like he didn't want to stop touching me. I didn't mind.

"You're new in town?" Cord turned down the sidewalk of the idyllic Main Street. "I'd have seen you before otherwise."

I thought of my trip to get here. How this place was so different from home.

No, this was my home now. At least for the short term, while I figured my life out. I hadn't heard from my parents yet, but I'd ditched my cell, so I was sure they'd blown it up trying.

"Yes." No way was I telling him anything else. Like how I'd run from the horrific surprise engagement party, gotten in my car, and driven until the cash I had in my purse ran out and I stopped in West Springs.

We made a left and a half block down, Cord stopped in front of a storefront and unlocked a door that read *McCaffrey Family Practice*.

"I really don't think I need medical attention," I protested weakly, still embarrassed over my klutziness. "It's just a scratch, and I'm sure the bleeding has already stopped."

"I will make sure." While his words were softly spoken, I could tell I wasn't going to be able to change his mind.

Cord tipped his head toward an examination room, and I followed. His office was geared toward kids, with a low shelf filled with books and toys.

I should have second thoughts about being alone in an office after hours with a stranger, but nothing about Cord felt off.

In fact, everything about him felt right. Besides, Bessie vouched for him.

The exam room was also kid-friendly, with large, framed posters of letters shaped out of animal bodies.

"Oh, I'm not in a hurry, I just hate to inconvenience you."

Cord's friendly dimples winked. "It's no trouble at all." He shocked me by placing his hands on my waist and lifting me up onto the table. The paper crinkled under my butt when I landed, and I blinked in surprise. Holy... wow. He was strong. I caught a whiff of his masculine scent—like pine and soap. The strangest need to lick him to see if he tasted as good as he smelled came over me.

Which wasn't like me at all.

Wow.

I'd thought I had no sex drive at all, and now I wanted to *lick* someone.

Maybe that was because of my pseudo-arranged marriage to Chester. He was handsome, but I hadn't been attracted to him.

This guy, Cord? My body was screaming *take me!*

He swiped antiseptic over my finger and examined the cut. "It's not deep, and it looks clean. I'll just put some antibiotic ointment on it and bandage it up."

I couldn't help swooning a little thinking of how comfortable he must make kids feel. He had that capability-porn thing going in spades. I watched as he applied the ointment and wrapped my finger with a soft, flexible bandage.

"So, Rachel, what brought you to West Springs?" He didn't move away when he'd finished. Instead, he remained inches from my body, leaning his hands on the examination table on either side of me.

"Oh, I, um, just sort of landed here," I replied.

Not a lie.

Cord waited for more. I didn't plan on telling him anything, but those green eyes were so compelling, I found myself spilling.

"I'm actually a runaway bride."

His body went still but he didn't step back. "Yeah?"

I swallowed, tried to clarify. "I mean, not even a bride. I'm not married. I ran away from an engagement party. You see, my family wanted me to marry this guy and be this person I don't want to be. They sprang it on me at the party, although I guess I went along for the ride for too long, even though I told my parents I wasn't interested in Chester. Then he got down on one knee with a ring and that made it real, so..." I took a big breath and kept on going. "Rather than just say no, which hadn't worked before, I ran. I think they got the message." I watched Cord's face as I dropped my crazy news to see how he would take my cowardice.

He appeared amused, perhaps not only from the story but my word vomiting. "You ran from the party."

I sighed, nodded. "Yes. I hitched a ride home, then got my car and drove off."

"You hitched a ride?" A muscle ticked in his jaw.

I held up a hand. "From a friend. The party was at the country club. A friend was leaving, and I asked for a ride. I didn't stick my thumb out by a gas station," I clarified.

He made a funny growling sound. "You left town."

"Yes. I barely packed a bag." I shrugged. "I drove and drove until the cash in my wallet ran out, and I wound up here."

He was quiet for a moment, then he nodded, as if figuring something out. "Fate. You're not married?"

"Not married, not even engaged."

He seemed to visibly relax. "This Chester has no claim on you?"

I shook my head, my hair swaying. "No. I'm taking some time away from the influence of my family to figure out what I want to do with my life."

Cord's brows lowered, then he glanced about. "Are you in some kind of trouble, Rachel? Is your family a danger to you?"

"No—nothing like that," I answered immediately, thinking of my mother and her charity lunches, and my father with his golf buddies. They wouldn't hurt me. Everything they did was out of love, I knew that, but I felt more like a *thing* for them than a person who had her own dreams. "I'm not up for dealing with my family or non-fiancé yet, that's all."

He studied me. "You will be safe here. I'll do anything necessary to make sure that happens."

I could only nod. What could I say about his obvious protective streak?

His body relaxed and he stepped even closer. This time, he tucked my hair behind my ear. "Well, you landed in the right place."

I gave a short laugh, although I shivered at the touch of his finger against my skin. It was a casual gesture, but it felt intimate. "You know, I think I did. I mean, I got lucky with the job at the diner. Bessie couldn't be more patient with me while I learn the ropes. Everyone who's come in has been really friendly."

He cocked his head to the side. "Do you have a place to stay? Do you need money while you get on your feet?"

My mouth fell open with surprise. "Wow. That is so kind, but no. I mean, yes, I have a place to stay, and no, I don't need money. I sold the pearls I wore to the party, and that was enough to rent an apartment Bessie told me about. So long as she doesn't fire me—

which, considering how bad I am, is a possibility—I think I'll be okay."

"She won't fire you." Cord's soft voice rang with confidence.

I looked at his clothing, which was probably still damp. "Maybe you didn't notice I just drenched a guy with ice water? Then tried to rub his crotch?"

Cord's smile grew broader and more lethal... to my panties. "Sweetheart, you can rub my crotch anytime."

A laugh rocketed from my throat before I could stop it. I covered my mouth with my hand, our gazes still inextricably connected.

"I want a date with you." He didn't ask.

My pulse sped up. Of course it was too soon, and yet I wanted to accept the offer with every cell of my body. Why did a few minutes with this man make me feel more than years with Chester?

"Um..." Why was it too soon? I'd made it very clear to Chester I didn't want to be with him, didn't even want to be in the same state. He had no hold over me. A hot guy was interested in me, and I was questioning?

What was wrong with me?

"There's a barbecue tonight that half the town will attend, Bessie included."

I was eager to make friends in this town, and didn't want to say goodbye to Cord McCaffrey. Still...

"What if I don't want to?" I asked him. It had never occurred to me to question before. And that was on me. The difference was, I wanted to be with Cord. I didn't want to go to my quiet apartment and be alone.

His eyes flickered with heat. "Then we'll do something else."

Butterflies filled my stomach. He really wanted to be with me. Me—clumsy, barely-ever-dated Rachel. He knew I was a terrible waitress, but had yet to find out the extent of my innocence. Just because I'd been paired off with Chester didn't mean I had any clue about men. Chester had barely kissed me. Dates had been dinners at the country club with our parents. The only time we spent alone was in his BMW.

He hadn't had to pursue me. I'd been a given. The trophy wife, perfect for his budding law career and political aspirations. I was untarnished. Perfect. Maybe that was why the whole thing drove me crazy. To Chester, I had been a sure thing as a wife. Except, I hadn't been a sure thing in bed. I wasn't naive enough to think that a man who was almost thirty like Chester didn't have needs. I knew he had to have slaked them with someone else if he didn't with me. I hadn't cared before. Hell, I hadn't wanted to know. I was just glad Chester hadn't been all that hot for me.

Which said everything. God.

But now, it was *very* important that Cord really be interested. In me. As a person. As a woman. Because I wanted to be more than smart arm candy. What was the phrase, *a lady in the streets, a freak in the sheets?* Maybe I didn't want to be a *freak,* but I wanted to be... sexy for a man. Desirable. Craved.

The way Cord was looking at me, I felt all of that.

"Sure, I'll go to the barbecue. Sounds fun."

His gaze raked over me, and heated. In my diner t-shirt and jeans, I probably smelled like the restaurant, and he was still interested.

"I'll be a perfect gentleman until you want that to change." His fingers played with the ends of my hair. I couldn't feel it, but still, I sucked in a breath.

I want that to change! I'd almost spoken the words out loud.

I didn't want to say no. "Okay."

"Great." Cord put those large hands around my waist again and lifted me from the table. He didn't let go right away.

No, I hadn't been hallucinating.

The guy was hella strong.

God, what a turn on that was.

Maybe he was right.

Maybe fate had led me to West Springs.

Even for a debutante like me, born with a silver

spoon in her mouth, things seemed to come together here.

Not the waitressing skills, but everything else. The job, the apartment. Bessie. Cord.

West Springs felt... right.

Cord felt right.

"Good. We'll go now."

"Now?" I shook my head. "No way. I smell like greasy French fries, and I'm wearing my diner clothes."

He leaned in and sniffed. "You smell perfect to me."

I flushed and pushed him away playfully. "I need to go home and change."

He nodded. "I'll give you a lift."

"No, um, my car is in the diner parking lot," I murmured as he steered me from the exam room. "Um, do I owe you anything?"

Not that I could pay, or dared use my insurance for fear my parents would track me.

"Don't be ridiculous," Cord scoffed. "Come on, I'll walk you." He settled a hand at my lower back and kept it there as he led me out of the building, locking the door behind us. We walked to my car and he opened the door for me and held it as I got in.

"Give me your address, and I'll come by in thirty minutes to get you."

"Thirty minutes?" I questioned. "A girl needs some time to look pretty."

He looked me over again as if he wanted to eat me up. "You're perfect as you are, but if you want extra time, then one hour. I can't resist a second longer."

A second longer.

Cord's deep rumble made me want to grip his shirt and pull him down for a hot, sloppy kiss. But that was crazy.

I was here to find myself, not a man. But Cord was quickly making me question that.

 ASH

"THANKS again for helping my mom with that huge armoire. You've earned this," Shelby said, handing me a beer bottle she'd just pulled from a cooler. It was ice cold beneath my fingers.

I took a swig, then followed her to the comfortable seating area on her huge deck. She dropped into a cushioned couch beside her mate, Ben, and leaned against him. He was big and broad, and Shelby fit perfectly beside him.

"No problem," I replied, thinking of the huge piece of furniture I'd brought from Marne's small house near Wolf Ranch to her new place here in West Springs.

"I wouldn't be surprised if she wants to be buried in it," Shelby added. I knew all about how sentimental Marne was for the thing. I'd heard the story about how she'd come to own it on our six-hour drive down from Montana.

The armoire was big enough to hold a body. Or two. It had been in the woman's bedroom, taking up one entire wall. Rand had helped me separate the two pieces and carry them out to my truck.

Marne, who lived here in West Springs now as well, had flown up to Cooper Valley as her house had finally sold. The large armoire had to be moved out. Instead of Shelby's mates leaving their pack here in Wyoming—Gibson was alpha and Ben was the enforcer—Rob Wolf had asked if I'd drive Marne and her prized piece of furniture to West Springs.

I'd grown up with both women within the Wolf Ranch pack. It was strange to see Shelby mated and settled in West Springs. She'd been so involved in our pack, and was missed, but everyone was glad she'd found her two mates. *Two!* For a while, she'd been the talk of the pack, but now that I was here among the Two Marks pack, it didn't seem unusual at all.

As for Marne, she'd worked hard for years after

her mate had walked out on her and Shelby, and it was good to see her settled as well—retired, and most likely waiting for grandpups. Gibson came outside, dropped down on Shelby's other side, and kissed her. She ruffled his salt and pepper hair. Yeah, I figured it wouldn't be long before Marne had several.

"I'm just glad I had help lifting it off the trailer. I might be shifter strong, but my back can't handle that kind of bulk solo." I was a carpenter and appreciated fine craftsmanship, but the armoire weighed a ton.

Ben laughed. "Your work is done. Put your feet up and relax." He pointed to the low table between us. I smiled, kicked back, and did as he said.

I had a beer in my hands, the scent of grilling meat in the air, and old and new friends surrounding me. All of the Two Marks pack had been invited to the alpha's house for a barbeque. While the reason was supposedly my visit, I had a feeling they had get-togethers often. Just like at Wolf Ranch. No reason needed. They were a tight pack.

While the weather was cooler, it was a beautiful fall day. There were heaters on the deck to keep the chill off, but pack members fanned out across the deck and onto the large backyard. Some played horseshoes, others had fun at corn hole, the bean bag tossing game. Gibson's brother, Landry, was manning the grill.

I'd learned he and his scent match, Wade, recently found their human mate. A wolf biologist, of all things.

I wasn't surprised, since the most recent matches at Wolf Ranch had been shifters mating with humans. Fate seemed to be interested in diversifying shifter genes.

"How are the babies?" Shelby asked.

I turned my gaze from the yard back to her. Audrey and Boyd had a little girl, Lizzie. Clint and Becky had Lily. I couldn't help but smile thinking of those two. "They're not babies as much as toddlers now. Both are walking every which way."

Those new matches were making their own families. Something I never had. No, that wasn't right. It was an insult to my grandparents, who raised me. They'd been older when I'd been left with them, and they'd died a few years ago—one after the other because as mates, they couldn't live apart.

I couldn't imagine being mated and having kids. I had no idea what to do. My grandparents had given me a loving home, but it wasn't the same as having a mom and a dad.

Shelby laughed. "I can only imagine what Boyd and Clint are going to be like when they start having males sniffing around their daughters."

My smile fell away. They weren't my little girls, but the idea of any guy even looking at them funny made my inner wolf snap. "Never gonna happen."

She laughed even harder. "What about you?"

I pointed to myself. "Me? Babies?" I'd never once considered myself ready to have kids. An uncle who gifted my friends' kids with noisy, destructive toys? Definitely.

"No. You. Mating," she clarified, rolling her eyes.

Gibson set his hand on her jean-clad thigh, and Ben had his arm around her shoulder. There was something about the three of them together that was appealing to me. Something... elemental. Rand, my best friend and partner in our construction business, had found his mate the previous summer. Fuck, it had been intense to watch. Rand was a possessive guy. To the extreme. Natalie seemed to like it, and they'd been hot and heavy ever since. But even that... intensity between them hadn't been a draw for me.

I didn't understand why until I saw Shelby with her mates when I arrived a little while ago.

Two males mated to a female. The connection, the bonding, was more. Powerful. This was why I didn't date. Not humans. Not shifters, especially knowing we weren't mates. I fucked as part of a full moon run release, but every time, something felt missing. I'd thought it was because the female hadn't been my mate. Because it was casual. Just sex.

Now I wondered if what I'd been missing was what they had here at Two Marks. What many of the guests at the barbecue had.

"Haven't found her," I replied, stating the obvious. It was impossible to keep it secret when a shifter found his or her fated mate.

If I had, though, would I still feel like something was missing? That there was a male who was supposed to be included? I had no idea how to even word what the three person relationship should be called. How did they even fuck?

As I took a swig of my beer, I watched Shelby and her mates. Wondered how they had sex. And that made me a creep, because I'd known Shelby my whole life, and I thought of her as a sister. Cousin, maybe.

"Work keeps me busy," I said, to fill in the silence, even though voices carried all around us. "Plus, without a mate or pups, I can help out like I did with your mom."

"You're welcome to stay as long as you want," Gibson offered. "Our connection with the Wolf family and pack is strong." He smiled down at his mate. "We're glad to have you."

I saluted him with my beer. "Thanks, but Rand

and I are starting a new project this week, so I've got to head back on Monday."

I hopped to my feet, not wanting to keep this line of conversation up. "Anyone want anything? I'm going to hit the spread inside."

People brought covered dishes to share. Between the grilled meats and the potluck offerings, the kitchen counter and dining table were covered.

Shelby, Gibson and Ben declined. After dropping my empty bottle in the recycling bucket, I headed in and found a plate. As I moved down the line of food, I froze.

There was a dish I smelled that I wanted. Sweet. Fruity. Turning around, I looked to the section where all the desserts were laid out to see what was so enticing.

A few cakes, brownies and cookies, but nothing that would make that delicious scent. I moved closer anyway, and took a deep breath. I turned again, away from the food, and into the great room.

My fists clenched and a growl rumbled in my chest. It wasn't food that awoke my wolf. It was the blonde woman who was looking at pictures on the mantle over the large fireplace. She was small and curvy, in jeans and a pale blue top. I didn't notice more detail than that because I couldn't look away from her face, even in profile. I approached as if my life depended on it.

Maybe I was a little aggressive or moved too quickly, because when she turned my way, her eyes widened.

When I was five feet away, I stopped. Barely. Yes, the scent was coming from her. Sweet and sugary, but human. *Definitely* human. I didn't know what she could be doing at a pack gathering like this but I didn't care. My mouth watered. My wolf stood and howled. I'd never acted this way with a female before. Never been drawn to one like there was a magnet pulling us. No, not a magnet. As if I'd been waiting for this moment. For her. Like...

Holy shit.

Like she was my mate.

"Hello," I said, my voice deep. It was almost impossible not to grab her and never let go. I knew I couldn't do that, I'd scare her, but the need was so strong.

This beautiful creature, whose eyes were the same pale color as her shirt, smiled.

"Hi," she replied. Her voice was soft. Gentle. "Is this your house?"

"Me? No. I'm visiting from another state."

"Me, too." She smiled, and that was it. Like a boxer hit by a wicked left hook, I was down for the count, and there was no getting up. I didn't want to. My fists clenched thinking about her sharing that smile with anyone else. It was mine. She was mine.

"I'm Nash." I moved closer now, not able to keep any distance between us.

"Rachel."

I was ready to take her hand and lead her to my truck—hell, toss her over my shoulder to get her there —and drive off and never look back. Maybe it was because I'd seen my friends run into their mates for the first time—their *human* mates—that I recognized that she didn't scent me. That meant...

Yup, human.

Rand had to be laughing right now. The same went for Boyd and Clint and the other guys who'd had to work their asses off to not only claim their female, but to make her fall in love with them.

Usually, claiming led to love, but since Rachel was human, I had to find other connections besides scent. Besides the DNA we clearly didn't share.

"I was getting myself a plate of food when I saw you. The potluck is impressive. Join me."

Impressive potluck? I sounded like an idiot. But I had to do something, say anything to engage. I remembered Rand and Natalie in the basement of her farmhouse before it burned down. When they crossed paths by the fuse box. He'd been as stupid for her then.

I didn't wait for her to answer, just took a gentle hold of her elbow and steered her toward the kitchen.

I was touching her!

I took a deep breath, tried to calm my aggression, but I only got more of her scent.

"I, um..." She looked toward the front door, then back at me.

"Did you forget your dish in your car?"

"No, I came with someone," she admitted.

My fists clenched again. I stopped in front of the long row of crockpots. Even over the bubbling scent of Swedish meatballs and cocktail hotdogs, I could tell she wasn't claimed.

"She can catch up," I said.

She shook her head, and her sleek hair swung back and forth. I stroked her cheek as I slid a few locks over her shoulder, then set my palm there. I felt her heat, her softness. Fuck, she was perfect. I smiled.

"I came with—"

"Me."

I turned my head at the sound of the deep voice.

I didn't move, but Rachel stepped back.

"Cord, this is Nash," she said.

This guy Cord wasn't looking at me. Or at Rachel.

He was looking at my hand that was still touching her. I didn't want to break the connection. No fucking way. This shifter would understand.

"Get your fucking hand off her," he snarled.

Or not.

"Cord!" Rachel said, backing up into the drinks area.

My fingers tingled, then curled into a fist at his harsh tone. He wanted me to stop touching my mate? I'd never felt so possessive in my life. I was irrational with it.

The guy was my height—heavier, though. Perhaps even broader through the shoulders, but I could take him. Especially now that I'd found Rachel. Nothing was going to separate us. He was shifter, I was sure. He had to know that she was mine, even if I hadn't fucked her and bitten her and claimed her.

"Find your own," I snapped.

Rachel gasped, and I mentally swore at how angry I was. I was scaring her. I didn't *scare* women.

Cord's jaw clenched. His eyes flashed amber and narrowed. "I have."

Rachel backed up again. "Um, guys..."

I stalked over to him so that Rachel would be behind me, and safe. Cord held his ground in the great room.

"Then go to her," I added.

"I have," he repeated, his gaze shifting to over my shoulder.

I frowned. He meant Rachel. My mate. Not his. "Not a fucking chance. I found her."

"I found her first," he repeated.

"You both need to stop. You're acting like second graders," Rachel scolded.

As long as Rachel was out of the way of the fight that was about to occur, I didn't give her too much of my focus. My mate was threatened. This shifter had no intention of hurting her, but he was claiming she belonged to him.

No fucking way. No one stole another shifter's mate. It was law.

I stared. He glared.

I heard Rachel's retreating steps and then the closing of the back door, her scent diminishing.

"The human is mine," I said when I knew she'd gone outside. Which pissed me off more. How much clearer could I get? "Back off."

Cord slowly shook his head. "She's mine. My mate. Her scent calls to my wolf."

I took a step closer. I wasn't backing down. "What kind of pack is this? You would dare argue with a shifter and his mate? She's mine."

He frowned, and his shoulders went back. "Who the fuck are you?"

This conversation wasn't going anywhere. We could finish it with fists. "Rachel's mate," I growled, then punched.

It landed on his jaw and his head jerked, but he was barely stunned. He moved quickly, knocking me back, we fell onto one of the oversized couches, then tipped onto the coffee table. It groaned beneath our joint weight. It slid across the wood floor as we hit the hard surface before we dropped to the ground. Something fell and shattered.

I was on top, so I struck again. Cord deflected, then flipped us, knocking something else over in the process. It smashed.

He got in a punch, and my lip caught on my teeth. It only riled me up, ready to take this shifter down.

"What the hell is going on in here?" The boom of the alpha's voice had us instinctively stilling.

We were breathing hard and glaring at each other, but the strong biological pull of authority made us dip our heads with respect.

"Shelby, take Rachel outside." It was Gibson, the alpha.

"But—" I heard my mate's voice, then Shelby's,

prodding her to agree. Rachel must have gone out to get Shelby, since this was her house.

"Get off me, asshole." I pushed at Cord. "My mate's leaving."

Cord popped up and swayed a little, but was stopped by Gibson with a hand on his chest. "Stay the fuck there, Doc."

Using the couch, I pushed myself up, wiping the blood from my lip with the back of my hand. It stung, but would be healed within a few minutes.

Gibson stood before us, hands on hips. Ben was behind him, waiting and watchful. No one else from the party was in the house—they were probably told by their alpha to remain outside. "Explain why you two are destroying my house."

"*He touched my mate,*" Cord snarled.

"*My. Mate,*" I countered, turning to face Cord to attack again.

"Enough." Even though Gibson wasn't my pack alpha, I couldn't do anything but still and obey. Only our ragged breathing could be heard.

The alpha took a step closer, and took a deep breath. His eyes widened, his nostrils flared, then he glanced back and forth between us.

"You're both right," he said.

"You're wrong," I said, then bit my cut lip. Had I just backtalked an alpha?

Gibson eyed me, but didn't do anything more than set his hands back on his hips.

"What do you mean?" Cord asked, which was what I should have said.

I frowned, looked to Cord. His hostility seemed to clear as he blinked and took a step back.

"Sniff. Figure it out," Gibson added.

We did. I didn't smell anything. "He doesn't have a scent," I said.

"No, he doesn't," Cord added.

Gibson ran a hand over his face. "For a doctor, Cord, you're acting like an idiot. You've been wishing you were scent matched. Well, it seems you are. Nash, here, is your match."

"What the—" Cord began, eyeing me now in a different way.

Holy shit.

"I have a scent match?" I asked. "No way. I'm not from here." This guy? A doctor? In West Springs? *A scent match?* That meant...

Gibson laughed. He came over, slapped us on the shoulders. "You two better figure your shit out—and fast, because you just drove your mate away. *Your shared mate.*"

4

 ACHEL

I HAD NEVER in my life witnessed anything so absurd. Grown men fighting over me?

I found her.

I found her first.

What did they put in this town's water, anyway? Testosterone? And here I'd thought Cord was a gentleman. More like a Neanderthal. And the other guy, Nash. He was the same way.

"Does that happen often around here?" I choked to the outdoorsy-beautiful young woman leading me out the front door. I glanced one last time over my shoulder. At the mess that had been made. At the two raggedly breathing men eyeing each other as if they wanted to go back at it.

The young woman laughed and stopped walking once we were away from the house. Their place was nestled back in the woods, but set in a pretty clearing. "No. Never. I guess they both found you irresistible. I'm Shelby, by the way. This is my place."

She indicated the giant log house we'd just left. It wasn't modern or fancy, but built with lots of rooms for perhaps a large-sized family who lived here originally. It was absolutely nothing like my parents' place in California. This place was lived in, a *home.* While my parents had parties often, they'd never think of having a potluck. The image was laughable.

"The growly guy who broke up the fight is Gibson, my boyfriend."

"I'm Rachel. I'm new in town."

She gave me a smile and raised her arms in the air. "Welcome to West Springs. Chaos and all. I've only been here a few months myself, actually. I'm from the same town as Nash. The guy back there—your second admirer? The blond hottie who couldn't take his eyes off you."

"Nash," I repeated, then blushed. "I don't think he saw me that way."

She came over, set her hand on my shoulder. "Oh, he saw you *that* way."

A thread of guilt ran through me at being as attracted to Nash as I was to Cord. What was it with me? The first two well-built men who gave me the time of day, and I wanted to drop my panties for both of them! Maybe I was the one who shouldn't drink the water.

It was like the sexual switch got turned on the moment I landed in West Springs. I went from no sex drive—because my only option to fool around had been Chester—to being attracted to two men in the course of a few hours.

"Nash is a great guy," Shelby said, interrupting my thoughts. She was probably a little older than me, but she seemed to have her life completely pulled together. A hot boyfriend whom she was living with. Me? I'd run away from home, and now I was a virgin who didn't know what to do with two men.

"We grew up together—he's like a brother to me," she added, like she was selling me on him.

"Um, yes. Cord seems great, too. I mean, I came here with him." I tried to assuage my guilt at finding Nash equally interesting.

Her eyes widened. "Oh. I mean, I know what happened in there but I didn't see you come in.

Terrible hostess, sorry. But I had no idea you came *together*."

"We met earlier, at the diner. That's where I'm working."

"So you came here with Cord and then ran into Nash. And then they fought."

I nodded. "Both of them said they found me, which is weird."

Shelby glanced toward the house and looked deep in thought. "Okay, wow. Yeah. I've known Nash forever, so I can vouch for him. Cord, I've only known for a short time, but he's great. The town doctor. There's no reason you can't have both." She sent me an impish smile.

My mouth fell open at the idea. Both? Me? I shook my head. "Oh, I-I could never. I don't want to lead a guy on just because I'm confused about what I want. And it isn't nice to come with one guy to a barbecue, and chat up another."

My mother had trained me to be ruthlessly polite. To smile and not stir up any kind of drama or fuss. It seemed I'd done both, without even trying.

She waved her hand as if that didn't matter. "What if you weren't confused?" Shelby challenged. A gleam came into her eyes, like she was planning something. "What if you really wanted two men?"

I frowned. I couldn't even find words to express to Shelby how outlandish her suggestion was. Two men.

She stepped in and lowered her voice conspiratorially, even though all the party guests were out back. The sun was low in the sky now, hidden by the trees, and the temperature was dropping fast, yet I was warm all over.

"Guys in this town are a different breed," she said. "There's actually quite a bit of polyamory here. I have two guys."

I was pretty sure my mouth dropped open and stayed that way. "What?" I tried to keep my tone neutral, but I could practically hear my mother's scandalized tone ringing in my ears.

"You met Gibson, but I'm also with Ben. We're in a relationship. I mean, we're practically married."

A slender woman with dark hair came around the side of the house. "Hey, Shelby. Mind if I join you?"

Shelby beckoned her over. "Caitlyn! Perfect timing. Come back me up, here. I was just telling Rachel—oh, Rachel, this is Caitlyn—that threesomes are a regular occurrence in West Springs."

"Oh, right. I heard two guys were fighting over a woman inside." She came to stand with us, making a little circle. Her dark hair was long and pulled back in a ponytail. She wore jeans and a Granger State sweat-shirt. I'd driven through Granger not long before I stopped in West Springs.

"That was me. Unfortunately," I said.

Caitlyn smiled. "Well, they'll probably work it out. Shelby's right, threesomes aren't unusual here." Even in the fading light, I could see her blush. "I have two amazing boyfriends."

I shook my head. "You ladies are blowing my mind right now. I can't believe this. You *both* have two boyfriends?"

I wasn't sure if I should feel like a total prude, or in awe. How did it even work? I had so many questions but I'd just met these women. I was sure they didn't want me asking how they had sex.

"I hate the word *boyfriend*. I mean, there's got to be another term, a better one, for what I have with Gibson and Ben. We live together, and we're committed long term," Shelby explained.

"Exactly. I'm with Wade, and Gibson's brother, Landry. It's weird, I know," Caitlyn said. "But this town has a long history of it, going back to early settlers who probably didn't have enough women to make a community without a little sharing."

Caitlyn looked to Shelby, who nodded. "Gibson and Landry are Wests. Their ancestors founded this town. The way I've heard them say it, if one husband died, the wife and kids were protected and cared for by the other one. I think it's romantic."

When it was worded that way, and from what I knew of the Wild Wild West, they made sense.

Caitlyn grinned. "All I know is that it's pretty wonderful from my standpoint. I get twice the attention." She waggled her brows and I laughed, my body suddenly flush with the inkling of what she meant.

I never even wanted one man's attention before, but now these women had me strangely craving two.

At the same time.

And that was just crazy. It was so not me. I'd never even really had Chester. Would he even fight another guy for me? I was convenient. Easy. Not something he... craved. It was clear Cord and Nash both *craved* me. Enough to fight over.

"Except Nash isn't from here, so it won't be an issue," I said, thinking aloud. "He said he was from out of state." I raised an inquisitive brow at Shelby for more information, since she was the one who grew up with him.

She nodded. "He's from Montana. He helped my mom move her favorite armoire down here, but I wouldn't be surprised if he decided to stick around."

"If the guys are into it, into *you,* keep an open mind about dating both of them," Caitlyn counseled. "I thought it was nuts at first, but I couldn't have chosen between Wade and Landry, and it seems to work perfectly for all three of us."

"There's no jealousy or weirdness?" I had a million more questions now. It was really hard to imagine how this sort of arrangement could work. I remembered sibling rivalry with my brother Kevin when we were kids. I couldn't imagine the rivalry between partners in a threesome.

Shelby answered. "Oddly, no. It all works out. That's my experience, too. But believe me, I was not on board in the beginning at all. I mean, I was attracted to both of them, but it also felt way too much. My guys are both dominant and possessive so I had to get used to the idea of having not one, but two intense mates— I mean, partners." She blushed and gave Caitlyn a look.

"They're possessive, but not with each other? In... in bed?" I still couldn't believe it.

"No. But that's where I think the West Springs history comes into play. They grew up with three-somes being normal," Shelby explained.

I glanced toward the house, wondering what was going on in there. I didn't hear anything. "You don't think they kept on fighting, do you?"

"No chance," Shelby said firmly. "Gibson wouldn't

allow it. I'm certain they are figuring out a way to share you right now."

A way to share me.

"But I barely spoke to Nash."

Both ladies shook their heads. "He doesn't need time to know he wants you," Caitlyn replied. "I mean, how long did Cord take? I bet not very long."

I laughed. "About five minutes."

They gave me the same look: *See?*

The thought shouldn't be so exciting. It shouldn't absolutely thrill me.

Just a little while ago, I was debating whether to even come to this barbecue at all, because I didn't need man complications. I had that back in California. But I'd come to the party with Cord and now I had *double* the trouble.

Yet happy butterflies flapped in my chest.

If there was such a thing as fate, and fate sent me to West Springs, could it be for this? For Cord *and* Nash?

The idea was ludicrous. I didn't even believe in fate.

Why, then, were my panties damp at the idea?

5

ORD

"THIS MAKES NO FUCKING SENSE," he said. *Him*. The guy who'd tried to take Rachel from me. My mate. Even with the revelation that he was my scent match, I was still seething at the fucker's audacity.

I tried to calm my breathing, but my wolf was still agitated. I was a doctor. I studied the DNA of shifters for inherited traits, but it made no sense to me either. This guy, Nash, sitting beside me, was my scent match. He wasn't even from our pack. All my research up to this point had indicated that scent matches only happened within the pack. I had a working theory that they developed due to proximity during puberty. But Nash had been nowhere near me growing up. So that theory just got blown out of the water.

"It's simple to me," Gibson replied.

After we'd cleaned up the great room—like little kids after making a mess—we'd gone into the alpha's office down the hall. The door was closed. The party went on outside. Rachel was somewhere, and not knowing where exactly made me twitchy and my wolf riled.

Gibson leaned forward, and set his forearms on the desk. "Doc, what does being scent matched mean?"

I tipped my head and eyed him, wondering if his question was serious. He was scent matched with Ben, and had found Shelby. He knew what the fuck a scent match was. Yet he was staring at me, waiting. Of course it was serious. He didn't joke. At least, not when he was in an alpha meeting. I grew up with his younger brother, Landry, and had known Gib long before he became alpha and leader of the Two Marks pack. Once he took over after his father's death, I respected and deferred to him. My wolf was powerless when it came to defying his command. Yet I could still be pissed.

"Scent matches share a certain amount of DNA,

including the gene associated with pheromone emission. This unusual phenomenon allows for true fated mate pairings to happen in duplicate—two males for one she-wolf, as the she-wolf is equally attracted to both males," I explained.

He nodded. "Exactly. From what I can tell," he tapped his nose, "you two are scent matched."

He'd already said the same thing in the living room, but it was taking a while to sink in. Instinctively, I took a deep breath. I picked up Gibson's scent, but not Nash's. I didn't know what mine was. A shifter couldn't pick up his or her own scent. And if I couldn't pick up Nash's, then—

Nash shook his head. "I just met my mate, and you're telling me I have to share her with him? I thought this scent matching was a Two Marks thing. I'm not from here."

Gibson studied him, quiet for a moment. "You sure about that?"

Out of the corner of my eye, I watched Nash's back straighten. His mouth opened and closed. "I-I..."

"To be scent matched, you have to be a pure Two Marks shifter," I clarified. At least, that's what my research had shown. I wasn't thrilled to possibly have that data proven invalid too.

Gibson knew this, but if he wanted me to point out

the obvious, I'd add more on. I didn't even know where Nash had come from, but it wasn't from around here.

"Something you want to tell us?" Gibson asked, still watching Nash.

"My parents died when I was young, and I was taken in by my grandparents in the Wolf Ranch pack. My parents were from Wolf Ranch. At least... I thought they were."

Holy. Shit.

Gibson pulled his cell from his shirt pocket, typed a message, then set it on the desk.

"I think it's time to make some introductions," Gibson continued. "Without fists. Cord, this is Nash Taggart. He's part of the Wolf Ranch pack in Montana. Like Shelby and Marne. He brought Marne back this morning from a visit."

I did my usual assessment when I first met someone. Usually, it was in my office for a medical visit. Nash was in his late twenties. Six-two. Two hundred pounds. Dark blond hair, cut short. Fit. Healthy.

"Nash, this is Cord McCaffrey. Medical doctor for the humans in West Springs and on rare occasions helps out with a shifter. Fortunately, it's been a while since we've had anything catastrophic."

Since his father had been crushed by a tree on a

full moon run. Years ago. I'd tried to help, but I hadn't even been a doctor then, and the injuries he'd sustained, even in wolf form, had been too grave.

Nash nodded in hesitant greeting. I didn't blame him. I wasn't too keen on meeting the guy either.

There was a knock on the door and Gibson called for the person to enter. It was Wade.

Gibson tipped his head toward Nash. "Wade, this is Nash Taggart."

Wade shook his hand while offering him an easy smile and a welcome.

"Wade's the head of IT at the distillery. I want him to look into your history. As alpha, I don't have to ask if it affects someone in my pack." Gibson glanced my way. Yeah, it affected me. "But I'd like your permission for him to dig around into your past. If you've got a scent match, it proves you've got Two Marks DNA. Pure DNA, meaning your parents were from here, and you probably have three, not two. My father, the previous alpha, would have known them, I'm sure. But I'm not the right generation."

"All right," Nash agreed with a stiff nod.

"Good."

"I've got your name. If you give me your birthdate, I can go from there," Wade said.

Nash shared it, and Wade left.

Gibson turned back to us. "There's a lot to be answered. One thing is clear. You two share a mate."

"I just met her," I told him.

"Me too," Nash added, his fingers clenching the arms of his chair.

Gibson held up a hand. "We're not starting this again. She's *both* your mate. I've never heard of scent matches never meeting before, especially before finding their mate. I have to say, this is a new one."

He shook his head and grinned. I had a feeling he was enjoying the novelty of this.

I sure as hell wasn't, and from the way Nash was glaring at Gibson, he wasn't either.

"I didn't even know the concept existed," Nash said. "At least, not until Shelby met you and Ben."

Gibson frowned. "That makes it complicated. You weren't raised with the concept of two males claiming a female together. In all ways. You ever fuck a shifter with another male before?"

Gibson was straightforward and blunt. By the way Nash's cheeks went ruddy, I knew the answer.

"In the Wolf Ranch pack, there are only pairs."

"That didn't answer my question," Gibson countered.

"No." Nash squirmed. "But it explains a lot."

"Such as?"

He pursed his lips, and I wasn't sure if he was open to sharing, or being compelled. "I've always thought something was missing. Several of my friends recently found their mates. Every one of them are good matches. Their love is powerful. But I always saw something lacking."

"A second male," Gibson said.

Shit.

Nash squirmed again. "It seems so. While you were in Montana with my pack, visiting with Shelby, we never met. It was only today, here."

Gibson nodded.

"I knew about you, your *unusual* match," Nash continued. "News spread through the pack about it, and how Shelby was claimed and moving here. Others found it unusual, I found it..."

"Familiar," I added for him.

For the first time, Nash looked at me without hostility.

"And you, Cord, have always known you didn't have a scent match," Gib said. "It's been an issue for you."

I nodded. If Nash was going to spill, I would too. Besides, Gibson knew it all anyway. "I didn't think I would be a good mate. I'm unable to reproduce."

I knew for a fact that I was shooting blanks

because I'd intensively studied the DNA of our particular breed of wolf. The breed that spontaneously produces scent matching in males so they can mate in pairs. Our breed was close to die-out so I'd, well, tested the DNA of anyone in the pack who was willing to contribute, and that included checking my own semen.

"The fact that I didn't have a scent match in the pack made me a poor choice for any she-wolf, fated or not. How could I claim my mate with no way to give her pups?" It had been a dilemma that haunted me. I'd become even more obsessed with the continuation of our species since I found out I couldn't contribute. I was broken, and had nothing to offer the pack or our future descendants in hopes of long term survival.

Gibson leaned back and clapped his hands, which startled me. I'd been caught in my constant loop of disappointment.

"Now you have your scent match. You can have pups. It's not as if matches know who the father of a pup is, or cares. Perhaps this is another reason for scent matches," he added, now sounding more like an inquisitive scientist than alpha. "You both," he glanced between us, "have your mate. Congratulations."

"Just like that?" Nash asked. "I find her, and have to share her."

Gibson narrowed his eyes. "Just like that. It's up to the two of you to figure this shit out. And fast."

"Because she's human," I added.

Gibson's dark gaze shifted to mine. "Exactly. You can't just fuck and bite her. She has no idea about shifters, and it's got to stay that way until you're sure you want to claim her."

"We do." Nash and I said it at the same time.

We looked at each other. We might never have met before, but we agreed on Rachel. We were claiming her.

Gibson stood. "Good. Then woo the shit out of her. Get her to fall in love with you. Then tell her what you are, and claim her. I don't want to see the three of you again until your scent is embedded in her skin."

He strode out, leaving us behind.

I eyed Nash. He stared at me.

"I'm not sorry I punched you," I said.

The corner of his mouth tipped up. "Me neither."

"What are we going to do?"

He pushed to his feet. "Find her, and never let her go."

I stood, and we shook hands. "I like your plan."

 ACHEL

THE FRONT DOOR opened and two large cowboys stalked out, each searching for, then honing in on, me.

"Here they come." Amusement rang in Shelby's tone. I was grateful that neither she nor Caitlyn abandoned me as the guys approached. Not that I was afraid. I just liked the female solidarity in the face of two hot-blooded men both apparently intent on *me*.

My heart picked up speed as they drew closer. I tried to detect whether there was still animosity between them, but I couldn't read anything in their expressions other than determination. Determination solely focused my way.

By the time they reached me, I was breathless because *two guys wanted me.*

"Rachel." Cord spoke first. "I apologize for my behavior inside. I hope you'll forgive both of us for acting like jackasses."

My gaze ping-ponged between the two men, who were both tall—and close enough, I had to tip my chin back to look them in the eyes. "Both of you?"

Was what Shelby and Caitlyn had suggested true? That these two men might want to *share* me?

Nash took off his cowboy hat. His blond hair curled, and was in need of a cut. "Yes, both of us. I was the real jackass. I just was so taken with you, I couldn't see straight." He winked, and my nipples tightened.

"So... the two of you worked things out?" I asked, hardly believing it. Based on the way they'd been throwing punches, I'd have thought they'd be cut up, but I didn't see a busted lip or swelling eye on either of them.

Nash shot a glance at Cord and nodded. "Yup. We came to an agreement."

I put my hands on my hips. "What's that?"

A sexy smirk flirted with the corners of Nash's mouth. "We have a proposition for you."

I heard one of the women gasp behind me, but didn't turn to look and see which one it was.

I cocked a hip, an unfamiliar sense of power coursing through me at being the center of attention for such attractive men. Men!

"We'll each give you a kiss, and you pick who will take you home. If you can't choose, you'll have both of us." Nash glanced Cord's way, and Cord nodded his agreement.

Shelby stepped closer and made a knowing sound —something like *mmm hmm*.

"I let both of you kiss me, and then I'm supposed to pick the best kisser?" I asked in disbelief. "Why does this sound like some kind of children's book? Will one of you turn into a frog at the end?"

Nash's grin grew wider. "Not a frog." He moved in close, not quite invading my space, but right on the edge. "Are you game, Rachel?" His voice dipped lower, and it was as much of a challenge as a question.

I licked my lips. I wasn't in California any longer. Two guys wanted me. Sure, I wanted to take some time and find myself, but wasn't this part of the journey? To find out what I liked in a guy? I had two who were willing to be guinea pigs. Or frogs. Whatever. I would be stupid to turn it down. Both men knew the score. I wasn't two-timing or cheating. Shelby and Caitlyn said it was a thing here, so it wasn't as if people were going to talk. Would I always wonder if I walked away from... them?

I took a deep breath, not believing I was going to do this. A few days ago, I was Rachel from California. Now, I was just plain-old Rachel. These guys didn't know I was rich. Didn't know where I was from, where I went to school, that my parents were overbearing with their love. They knew nothing but had the basest of interest in me.

And I liked it.

"I'm game." My voice came out sounding rusty.

Nash stuck his hand in his pocket and withdrew a quarter. "Heads or tails?" Sliding a glance at Cord, he flipped it in the air.

"Heads."

Nash caught the quarter and slapped it on the back of his wrist. All five of us leaned in to see the reveal. "Heads, it is."

Goosebumps raced across my skin as I turned to Cord, but I gave Nash a quick glance. Suddenly, I was a little nervous that they'd throw punches again. But he only gave me another wink. "My turn soon, beautiful."

This was crazy. I felt like a schoolgirl playing Spin The Bottle or Truth Or Dare, but nothing in the world could drag me away from this experience.

How easy would it be to choose? I couldn't decide if I was hoping for a clear winner, or for a tie. I didn't want to hurt anyone's feelings, and I definitely wanted to try kissing two different guys. My only experience had been Chester, and that was like kissing a cold fish.

A tie.

Oh God, I actually wanted a tie!

Caitlyn and Shelby nudged me toward Cord, who came close with all the confidence and swagger of a bull rider. He reached out and cupped the back of my head, drawing my face to his as he leaned down. My breath caught, but he stopped just when my eyes were about to flutter closed, and met my eyes for one searing moment.

The heat and glow to his golden gaze sent tremors of excitement down my legs, curling my toes.

"Hi," he murmured.

I almost swooned.

My panties soaked with arousal. I felt like a goddess, more beautiful, more worshipped, more honored than I'd ever felt in my life.

"Hi," I whispered back.

Cord closed his eyes, and he brought his lips to mine.

There were whoops and cheers from Caitlyn and

Shelby, and words of encouragement, like we were in a sports competition and needed to be egged on.

I grasped Cord's strong arms to steady myself, rising up on my toes to meet him. He went slowly. Just a brush of his lips across mine. Then another. He slanted his mouth and tasted me. Then it was like he lost control. He wrapped an arm behind my back and yanked my body flush against his while he devoured my mouth. His tongue swept between my lips, he twisted and sucked and demanded I give him every-thing—every ounce of passion I never knew I had inside me.

And I gave it.

It poured out of me. I returned the kiss with a fervor, a desperation for more. I melded my body to his. If I could have crawled up him like a tree, I prob-ably would have. As it was, I lifted one leg and slid it along the side of his, like I was offering up my core. Like we were having sex, standing up and fully clothed.

I wanted him that much.

I didn't care about Caitlyn and Shelby. I forgot about Nash. It was just me and Cord, and the Wyoming mountains spinning and circling us like cameras on a movie shoot.

Cord's grip on me tightened. He shifted to move

his forearm under my ass and boost my legs around his waist.

"All right, Doc." Nash's voice, which seemed to come from far away, held a thread of irritation. "I'm cutting in," he growled.

"Ding-ding-ding," one of the women said, as if to end this round like it was a boxing match.

Cord broke the kiss, but didn't let go of me. We stared at each other, panting like we'd finished a marathon. I could have sworn his eyes glowed amber. His face was flushed. There was a wildness to him that I hadn't seen before, and it made me want to tear off my clothes and let him devour me.

"Mmmm," Shelby said appreciatively.

"An excellent showing from Contender Number One," Caitlyn narrated.

"Wow," I murmured, ignoring the peanut gallery.

No offense to Nash, but I highly doubted he could top that.

Which was good. I'd come with Cord, I should leave with him. I hoped for an easy, clear decision.

I almost told Nash right then—to save him the embarrassment of losing—but Cord shocked me by turning me around to face Nash. He kept his hands on me possessively, but also seemed to be offering me to his rival.

Instead of taking me from Cord, Nash stepped forward, pressing me back and sandwiching me between him and Cord.

"I'll have some of that," Nash murmured, the irritation gone from his voice, replaced only by appreciation. Fascination.

He cradled my head in both his hands, his thumbs caressing my cheekbones, and leaned in for his kiss.

Cord didn't let go. His hands rested lightly on my waist but when Nash claimed my mouth, he stroked them down my hips, one hand moving to massage my ass.

I responded—not sure if it was to Nash's kiss or Cord's stroking, or the combination of the two.

My body heated and ached. Nash deepened his kiss and I became the aggressor, slipping my tongue between his lips, demanding more. I loved kissing him just as much as I had Cord—even more now, because Cord was a part of it, stoking my pleasure as Nash gave it to me.

I liked two sets of hands on me.

My brain cells shorted out—I could hardly grasp what I was doing, making out with two men at once!— but my body? My body knew everything, even though I'd never done *anything*. Every carnal instinct flared to life. I wanted it all. Needed it. Two men desired me, and I wanted them both.

Nash didn't so much break the kiss as move it. He tipped my head back and dragged his open mouth down the column of my neck until his teeth lightly scored my shoulder.

"Ding-ding-ding," our referee said softly, like she was also moved by the kiss and hated to stop it.

"Easy, friend," Cord advised, catching Nash by the hair and lifting his teeth away from my skin. His tone wasn't aggressive or angry. I would swear it was like the two of them were on the same team now. Team Make-Rachel-Theirs.

Which didn't make sense.

How could two strangers suddenly agree to share a woman?

Even if one of them was from a town where it was common, it seemed too far-fetched to believe.

Yet it was happening.

Nash rubbed his thumb over the place where he'd nipped my skin. "So what's the verdict, beautiful?" He didn't seem worried.

Neither did Cord, who wrapped an arm around my waist and held my body against his. Nash touched me from the front, his hands lightly running over me—down my arms, along my sides. He picked up one of my hands and kissed the inside of my wrist.

I blinked, my mind mush.

Did they expect me to pick both?

Where was that sense of competition they'd had inside the house?

I licked my lips. "It's a tie." My voice didn't sound like my own. It was husky. Sultry. Complete foreign.

"I knew it!" Shelby declared with glee.

"A win for all three," Caitlyn agreed, clapping.

Shelby came over to stand at my side. With guys front and back, I turned my head to look at her. "You okay?" she asked.

I nodded.

"You're new here. Even though they might be amazing kissers and make your eyes all blurry like that," she pointed at me, "you don't have to leave with them. You can stay as my guest. I can give you a ride home. You're in control."

I appreciated her level headedness when I was anything but.

"She's right," Cord murmured.

"You're in control," Nash repeated.

What did I want? To go back to my little apartment all alone? Stay with Shelby and Caitlyn? Let Cord and Nash drive me home and then...

I flicked my gaze to Nash. He was watching me closely, those blue eyes intent. Patient.

"I'm good with the guys," I told Shelby.

She smiled. "Yeah, you are. Have fun, ya'll." She gave a little finger wave, then she and Caitlyn faded away, leaving the three of us to our... threesome.

Oh my God, I was going to have a threesome. Except, I didn't even know how to have a twosome. I wasn't clueless. I had been to college, lived in a sorority house. I'd used vibrators, but they weren't the real deal. These guys were.

"Um, guys?" I said. "There's something you should know."

Neither man had moved away from me. I was still sandwiched firmly between the two of them, their hands everywhere, their heat engulfing me.

"What is it, beautiful?" Nash asked.

"I'm a virgin."

7

*N*ASH

RACHEL WASN'T the only virgin among us. Oh, I'd had sex before, but never like this. Never with an audience, and never with another guy. No, I wasn't attracted to Cord, or any male, for that matter. But I'd never had a threesome—at least the kind that it appeared I was going to be in, and which was prevalent within the Two Marks pack: two males and a female. Two males who desired not each other, but the female.

Naked.

Together.

As in: *very* together.

"How does this work?" Rachel asked as Cord pushed the button on his visor to open his garage door.

Instead of taking her home as first planned, Cord had suggested his house, since it was bigger. I assumed he meant the bed, specifically. Rachel had agreed without taking any time to consider. While she couldn't scent us, she seemed calm about going home with two men she'd just met. I had no idea what Shelby and the other woman had told her while we'd been holed up with Gibson, but it hadn't been anti-threesomes. It seemed they'd given her a little pep talk. Either way, she obviously felt the connection even while being human.

She was the virgin, but I was the nervous one. That kiss... fuck me, that kiss had been amazing, but that's all it was. No matter how much I wanted to strip her bare and put my mouth on every inch of her, she wanted Cord, too.

I'd never been with a female who also wanted someone else. I'd actually never been with a human, either. So she was my first in several ways.

"You mean more than kissing?" Cord asked.

She nodded and her blonde hair slid over her shoulders. With her wedged between us in Cord's truck, we touched along our sides. For my wolf, it wasn't enough. My dick was hard, had been since the kiss in Shelby's front yard. Cord's words... the idea of more, made me shift in the seat.

"Yes," she replied, her voice soft in the cab.

Cord had shut the music off as soon as he started the engine. He'd pointed out various things as we came down the mountain. Rachel and I were both new to town. I didn't pay him much attention. It was all I could do to handle her sweet scent in the closed cab. I had to assume Cord was doing it so he didn't pull the truck over and fuck her on the side of the road.

I'd planned on rolling out of town on Monday, but the moment I scented Rachel, that plan had changed. It looked like West Springs would be my new home town, so long as Rachel was in it. Although, I had shit to figure out. I had a business. A house. Friends. All of that with a different pack, and in a different state.

Rachel had mentioned she was visiting from out of state too. Where? Who was she visiting? It hadn't been Cord—at least initially.

A lot of questions, but now wasn't the time to work through them.

"We're both going to make you feel good," I told her. It wasn't a statement but a vow. "But there's no pressure. We won't do anything you're not ready for. We can kiss all night like we did."

Her cheeks turned a pretty pink and she looked down at her lap. "I told Cord that I left home because of an overeager boyfriend."

I stiffened. "Overeager how?" I asked, my voice laced with anger. I was ready to track down this asshole and rip his head from his body. I was overeager, but I'd never touch her without consent. Ever.

She set her hand on my clenched fist, obviously recognizing my fury. "Chester and I were thrown together as a pair since... forever. I went along with it, and that's my fault. I didn't think much of it while I was in college because I was away, and he wasn't around. He lived his life, and I lived mine. Then I graduated and moved back home. He decided it was time to move things along—my parents were in on it—since they had a surprise engagement party. Well, I was the only one who was surprised."

"You're engaged?" Holy fuck, I wouldn't have touched her if I'd known. I didn't see a ring on her finger.

She shook her head. "No. God, no. I left the party. The club. The state. I'm not marrying Chester. He's not really a boyfriend."

"Why not?" I wondered. Shifters didn't have

boyfriends or girlfriends. Maybe there was something to this human behavior I didn't understand.

"Because he never once made me feel the way you two do," she admitted.

Fuck. My dick spurted pre-cum knowing that she found pleasure in our kisses.

I spared Cord a glance as he pulled the truck into the garage. Night had fallen, and I could see his face with my night vision. His jaw clenched as his gaze met mine.

I'd barely met the guy but I could read his mind. This was right. Rachel was our mate. No wonder she'd felt something with us and not the fucker from home. She may be a human, but we were the males for her. No one else.

"Do your parents know where you are?" I asked.

She shook her head. "Not yet. It's only been a few weeks, and I need to take some time to figure out what I want, not what they want me to be."

"What's that?"

She shrugged. "A country club wife to Chester. Mother. Charity organizer. Pretty much: my mom."

"You don't want that?"

"A mom, yes. Someday." Cord stiffened as she spoke. "The rest, no. But I don't know exactly what I want either. I've let them dictate my life for so long, I didn't even notice why I was so unhappy."

"What do you want?" Cord asked.

"This." She bit her lip. Her cheeks flushed prettily once again. I wondered what other places were that pink color. "I want to live a little. Experience it on my own terms. The tips I made at the diner is the first money I've ever earned. It feels good to stand on my own two feet, even though I'm a terrible waitress."

Cord laughed. "Rachel works at the diner on Main," he explained. "We met earlier when she—"

"I spilled a glass of water on him."

"Ice water," he clarified. "A good thing, too, because my dick was so hard for you."

She gasped and whipped her head around to stare at him. He nodded.

"Like now. But I don't want it to go down. I want you to stroke it. Lick it. Suck it. Maybe even fuck it."

She shivered, even though it was far from cold in his truck. I took a deep breath, not only because I wanted exactly what Cord had said for myself, but to breathe in her scent. It was different now. Darker. Richer. Fuck, she was aroused.

"Are your panties wet, beautiful?" I asked, reaching up and stroking her hair. I couldn't help touching her.

She bit her lip and nodded.

Over her head, I eyed Cord. Yeah, we were in agreement. Time to move this out of the truck and make our mate scream until she was hoarse.

I was strangely and fiercely proud of the three of us. Rachel had known her life wasn't as she wanted it and left, seeking more. Well, she'd found it.

"Good." I took her hand and set it over my dick. Her eyes flared as she felt how hard I was through my jeans. "I never felt like this before either," I said. "I know you asked how this works, but I'm new to three-somes too. I've never been in one. This feels right though."

Cord didn't look like he was sweating bullets. Except, he knew about the Two Marks way. On full moon runs here, did two shifters fuck a female together? For fun and to let off steam, like I did solo? Had he done this before or were we all going to be fumbling?

Cord turned off the truck and hopped out. "Let's go inside."

She gave him a dazzling smile, then nodded.

Cord turned and stared at us. I blinked, realized I was being a dumbass. Rachel couldn't easily slide past the steering wheel. I got out on my side and held out my hand for her to take.

The feel of her fingers beneath mine sent a zing

right to my balls. I saw the bandage on her hand. "What's this?"

She gave it a glance, then rolled her eyes. "Nothing. Just a little cut because I'm clumsy."

I didn't like to see her injured, even in the smallest of ways, especially since she didn't heal like shifters. But if she played it off as nothing and Cord wasn't looming over her in doctor mode, I let it go.

"Come here, beautiful. I need another kiss."

She wrapped her arms about my waist and tipped her chin up. I loved the open invitation, and put my mouth on hers. I growled at her sweetness.

I cupped her butt and lifted her up, and she wrapped her legs around my waist. I didn't stop kissing her. I couldn't. Hell, no.

"This way," Cord said. I had to open my eyes to see he'd opened the door to the house and was holding it wide for me to pass through.

He led the way out of a mud room, through the kitchen, down a hall and into his bedroom, flipping lights on as he went.

I sat down on the edge of Cord's bed with Rachel in my lap. She lifted her head, blinked her eyes open, and studied me.

"I think Cord's lonely," I said, surprising myself that I was willing to pass her off.

She looked over her shoulder. He'd dropped into a comfortable leather chair in the corner, knees spread and forearms on the arm rests. He looked relaxed, like he was watching a favorite TV show instead of another shifter making out with his mate on his bed.

"Go give him some sugar, too."

I patted her butt and she climbed off my lap.

Fuck, this was hot. And for some reason, I was even more aroused as she settled into Cord's lap and they started kissing. It was so hot, I had to let my dick out, carefully opening my zipper and tugging myself free.

I sighed in relief, then gripped the base and watched.

I barely noticed the tan walls. The dark wood floors. The cold fireplace beside Cord's chair. How the room was neat. I didn't want to look away, but I assumed the bed was huge. If Cord was a Two Marks shifter, he'd expect just this scene at some point.

They kissed. They groped. Soon, Cord got her top off.

I did everything I could to stop myself from going over to them and getting my hands on her. I wanted to cup her breasts, nibble along her neck... take a little bite.

Her skin was pale and creamy in the soft light, and

the lacy red bra made her look anything but innocent. Because that thing wasn't demure. It was sexy as hell, with cups that supported more than they covered, and straps that did absolutely nothing but make me groan and stroke a little harder.

"You still good?" Cord asked, his hands sliding up and down her sides, but his gaze shifted from her eyes to the swells of her breasts.

"I might be a virgin, but I'm not completely clueless. I... I have toys. A vibrator."

I groaned, picturing her naked in bed, her thighs parted and her getting off to a thick vibrating dildo. That was never happening again.

"You put it inside you? Fucked yourself with it?" Cord asked.

Gibson had said Cord was a doctor, which meant he wasn't shy about talking about the body.

"Yes. If you're worried about it hurting—sex, I mean—it won't," she replied.

I grinned. "Beautiful, were any of your toys this big?"

She looked at me over her shoulder, then dropped her gaze to my lap. Her eyes flared wide. Yeah, as I thought. I was big and while I didn't want to hurt her... ever, her tight pussy might have been opened up by some silicone, but it had never experienced a real dick.

Or two. I couldn't wait to watch her face as I filled her to the brim.

"No. Can I... can I touch it?"

I swallowed, then wiped a spurt of pre-cum with my thumb. "Beautiful, you can do anything you want with it."

She glanced at Cord, who nodded, then she climbed off his lap and came over to me. Dropped to her knees. Licked her lips.

Cord growled.

Holy fuck. *This* was what I'd been missing my whole life.

8

RACHEL

THIS WAS CRAZY. Absolutely nuts. I was about to punch my V-card with not one, but two hot men.

Whom I'd just met today.

Except they didn't feel like strangers. They felt familiar in ways I couldn't understand. They were protective and tender and attentive as hell. The fact that they'd fought each other for me...

Swoon.

I'd given Chester exactly one blow job. Well, a *partial* one. He'd just graduated college. I was a senior in high school. I'd gotten tipsy at a charity ball and we were tucked away in the back corner of the cloakroom. I'd just figured out how to get him in my mouth when someone came for their coat.

We'd both been so mortified, we never tried to do anything again.

That's what I told myself, anyway.

Now that I was looking at Nash's cock, though, I knew that wasn't true. I just hadn't been attracted to Chester. Because the moment I gripped the base of Nash's cock, my hips writhed with pleasure. Need. I licked around the head of it, paying attention to the cleft at the base, then teasing the slit with my tongue. I'd seen enough porn being in a sorority—and hearing the other girls talk—to know what to do. A bead of pre-cum formed and I tasted Nash's essence, salty and warm.

Nash's breath was uneven. His fingers burrowed into my hair. I lifted my gaze to meet his. His blue eyes glowed in the lamplight, and his nostrils flared. "Don't stop." He already sounded desperate. Wild.

A sense of power flowed through me. I'd felt weak my whole life. While protected by my parents, I'd also been guided, molded, shaped to their wants and dreams. The perfect Stepford daughter. West Springs made me feel like a new person. These men did.

I never would have done anything so wild or bold

before, and it had a lot to do with Cord and Nash themselves. I hadn't been interested in other single guys I'd met. Only these two.

I took Nash into my mouth, reveling in the velvet steel of his length. He was huge, so I slid him into the pocket of my cheek, bobbing my head over his manhood and sucking hard as I pulled back.

"Fates, Rachel," he growled. His fingers curled in my hair, tugging hard—then, as if he realized his strength, gripping gently.

I moaned around his member. Knowing Cord was watching—feeling the weight of two heated stares— made it all the hotter. I squirmed, wanting some kind of friction on my clit.

Cord must have read my mind, because he moved and knelt on the floor behind me. While I swirled my tongue along the underside of Nash's length, Cord unbuttoned my jeans and slid his hand inside my panties from the back. I arched, humming around Nash's huge cock.

"Does that feel good, beautiful?" Cord murmured. He brushed a finger over my wetness, teasing me open. No one had ever touched me before, and it was... God.

I attempted to make an *mmm hmm* sound without coming off Nash's dick. Nash reached inside my bra cup and toyed with one of my nipples. I sucked him harder, with more enthusiasm than I knew was possible.

My body was feverish, needy, yet all I cared about was making Nash feel good. I'd never wanted to succeed at something so much in my life. I may not have found myself yet, but I certainly was discovering a new side to me.

"I'm already a goner," Nash growled. "I can't hold back, beautiful."

"Do you want Nash to come in your mouth?" Cord asked, his breath fanning my neck. "Or on those pretty tits?" He unfastened the back of my red bra and it slid down my arms.

God, I'd never gotten this far before. I'd heard the big debate about spitting versus swallowing, but honestly wasn't sure if I was ready for that. I popped off and cupped my breasts, looking up at Nash. I licked my lips and stared at his glistening, engorged dick.

"Aw, fuck, Rachel. That's the prettiest thing I've ever seen." He gripped his dick and pumped it hard, his face already contorting with his imminent orgasm. I smiled. I'd made him this way.

Cord gave my ass a light slap with his free hand, and I came up off my heels. "She's a dirty little virgin, isn't she?" He slid his hand into my panties further and found my clit.

I cried out, gripping Nash's thighs for stability the moment Cord touched me there. It was crazy, but I was ready to come, too. Just from a few light touches and sucking Nash off.

Nash let out an animal-like growl of pleasure and angled the head of his cock at my chest. "Coming!" he choked. His seed arced and spilled across my breasts at the same time as Cord applied more pressure to my clit, gripping my hip to steady me with his free hand.

"Yes!" I cried, not sure if I was cheering Nash on or claiming my own victory. My hips bucked, and I dropped my own hand between my legs to help Cord press me the way I liked it. I rode both our hands as my orgasm stormed through me, fast and frantic, and over too quickly.

It was a release but I already wanted more.

I wanted the real thing.

Penetration with a real cock, not just having hot seed spurted across my chest.

How I knew that was beyond me, but I was never more sure of anything in my life. I needed sex.

Right. Now.

I looked over my shoulder at Cord as I hooked my

thumbs in the waistband of my jeans and tugged them down.

"Do you need more, beautiful?" Cord choked, his eyes taking on an amber glow.

"I need you," I said, wriggling to get my pants off. I needed him now.

"Fuck, that's hot," Nash said, helping me stand to kick my feet free. He dragged his fingertips between my breasts, down the center of my belly to the top of my panties. "You always wear a matching bra and panties, little virgin?" he asked. The tension in him was gone. A smile curved his lips. His jeans were open, and his dick was out. And still hard.

"Yes." I laughed. "I like them to match. And you're going to need to find a new name for me soon."

Nash bent his head and flicked his tongue over my nipple, as Cord dragged my panties down my legs.

"Do you have a condom?" Nash asked Cord. There was no aggression to the question. I liked the way they seemed to work together to keep me satisfied and safe. I didn't sense competition or awkwardness.

"A condom, yes. Thanks for the reminder." Cord went to the bathroom as Nash continued to suck and tease my nipples. This was Cord's house. By the time he returned with a string of foil packets between his fingers, I was arching my back, moaning for more of Nash's mouth.

"She's so ready," Nash said to Cord, his voice thick. "Her scent is driving me wild, even though I just came."

My scent? I hadn't used any perfume after my shower—I wasn't a fan of chemical fragrances, preferring essential oil blends instead. Hopefully I didn't smell like grilled onions.

"I know," Cord agreed.

I didn't get it, but I was beyond caring. Cord had stripped off his shirt and the sight of his bare torso made me want to throw myself at him. In fact, I practically did. I turned to face him and wrapped my arms around his neck, bringing my lips to his mouth.

We kissed, and Nash—still sitting on the bed—slid his fingers between my legs from the back, opening the cleft of my ass with his thumb. I bucked my hips at the sensation.

"Why don't you go back to your chair, Cord, and she can climb on top for her first time."

Cord must have liked the suggestion because he walked backward, taking me with him. "Does that sound good to you, beautiful?" he asked, breaking the kiss.

I nodded, watching as he unbuckled his belt, then

his jeans, dropping them to the floor in a heap, along with his boxer briefs.

He was just as well-endowed as Nash. A bit longer, but not as thick, with an angle to the left. He sat back in the armchair, ripped a condom off the strip, and rolled it on his erection. I straddled his lap, my knees resting on the cushion outside his thighs.

He gripped my hips, holding me aloft with that same strength that had surprised me back at his clinic. "Take my cock, beautiful." His voice sounded thick, like he could barely hold back. "Rub it over your slick little pussy until it slides in."

I obeyed, stroking myself with the head of his sheathed cock until it settled in the notch and my flesh parted. It didn't hurt, but it was a stretch, even having used toys before. My breath stopped, and Cord used his strength to hold my weight and keep me from fully seating over his member.

"Take your time," he coached. "We go at your pace, sweetheart. Make it feel good."

I did. I relaxed and took him deeper, inch by inch, until I made contact with his thighs and could grind my clit down on him.

"That's it, beautiful." He slowly guided my hips tighter, tugging me against him, then back, keeping my clit in contact with his root the entire time.

"Oh God," I moaned.

"That's so hot," Nash said from the bed.

I looked over my shoulder at him, wondering if he felt left out. Even though he'd already come, his dick was hard and he was stroking it.

"Do you want to join in?" I asked. I didn't know the protocol for threesomes, but I couldn't stand the idea of disappointing either of these men. I had a dick in me for the first time and I was clenching it, trying to adjust.

"I just wanna watch." Nash's voice sounded as thick as Cord's had. "I've never seen anything so beautiful in my life."

"You're okay with Cord having sex with me?"

"Cord, yes. Fuck, it's such a turn-on watching his dick sink into you."

Knowing Nash found us beautiful made it all the more arousing. Not that I wasn't already in the throes of the most erotic sensations I'd ever experienced. Being filled by Cord felt like a freaking life purpose. How could I have thought sex toys could deliver satisfaction? Nothing—*nothing*—compared to this. I turned back, and Cord's gaze met mine.

Sweat dotted his brow and I had to imagine holding still was costing him. I lifted and lowered, gasping at the delicious sensations. Then I closed my eyes and let go. I rode Cord, dizzy with lust, drunk with pleasure. My head lolled around on my neck, my breasts bounced, I arched my back. It all felt so perfect. So delicious.

Then it became not enough. A sense of urgency washed over me. I ground down harder on Cord and he pulled and pushed my hips faster, letting me ride him at the speed that matched my new need.

It still wasn't enough, and I whimpered.

I needed more. Oh God, I was desperate.

"She's ready to come," Nash observed.

I was. I was definitely ready.

"So am I," Cord choked. "But it's so good, I don't want it to end."

"I know what you mean," Nash said. His voice sounded closer. And then he was behind me, lightly cupping my breasts from behind as I rode Cord. "Can you wait for Cord, baby?" he murmured, his hot breath feathering across my ear.

"Yes," I gasped, only partly sure what he meant.

"Good girl." He kept his face close to mine. "Cord's getting close."

He was right. Cord was losing control. His face contorted with pleasure, a muscle jumping across his cheek as he opened his mouth. He pumped his hips up to meet mine, his butt leaving the chair to drive deeper into me as he yanked my hips over his lap.

On the third rough pump, he shouted and his eyes flashed gold.

"Now, Rachel," Nash urged, pinching both my nipples at the same time.

My pussy clenched around Cord's cock and a second, far more powerful orgasm ripped through me.

This one was incredible.

Life changing, actually.

If I'd only known what had been missing from my life, I would have broken up with Chester and had sex long ago.

No. That felt wrong.

Because I wouldn't ever want to give up this first time. Right here. Right now. With these two perfect men.

When the last tremor passed, I went limp, flopping down against Cord's chest. One of the men stroked my hair—Nash, maybe.

"Let's get her into the shower," Nash murmured, and somehow Cord stood from the chair with me still glued to him. I wrapped my legs around his waist and he followed Nash into the bathroom. He lifted me off his dick, and I hissed at the feel of emptiness. He rid himself of the condom as Nash stepped into the huge walk-in shower and turned on the water. Then he stripped bare. Once he'd tested the temperature, he stepped in, then Cord and I joined him.

The water fell over the three of us and I closed my eyes, sandwiched between two sexy cowboys.

This was a dream. It had to be. It was too weird not to be.

Any minute, I'd wake up and it would be over. I'd have to face my life and figure out what I wanted from it. It certainly couldn't be two men. That didn't happen.

But until that happened, I just wanted to soak it all in.

 ORD

AFTER WE WASHED RACHEL, I left Nash to help her dry off while I rustled up some food.

We'd been too impassioned to leave the barbecue and jump in the sack to grab any food, and I'd heard Rachel's stomach growl in the shower. The urge to feed her, to take care of all her bodily needs, nearly made my wolf frantic.

I pulled out a loaf of bread and some turkey slices and went about making bacon, turkey, avocado sandwiches—my personal favorite. It was strange that my wolf felt settled enough to leave my unmarked mate, even for a moment, but I supposed that was because Nash was with her. It said something that my wolf trusted Nash, because after his display of aggression back at Gib's house, I wasn't entirely sure. And unlike other shifters in the pack who'd known their scent mate for years, I'd known him for a few hours.

A wolf's biology didn't lie though. If Nash was Rachel's mate, he'd do everything in his power—including kill or die—to ensure her happiness, safety, and sexual satisfaction. I was concerned about the fact that he hadn't been raised in West Springs and didn't know our ways, but biology should take care of that, too. As my scent match, cooperation with me for Rachel's happiness should be hard-wired into him.

We may have had a rocky start—hell, that was an understatement—but the fact that we settled our differences and came together to satisfy our mate was a testament to Nash's Two Marks genes.

"Need any help?" Nash asked, appearing in the kitchen, holding our mate's hand. He was in just his boxers and she was wearing my t-shirt. Her blonde hair was damp and she looked sexy as fuck. I shouldn't care that she'd been a virgin, but my wolf howled knowing I'd been the first to get in her. Nash would have his turn soon. We were far from done.

"I wasn't prepared for guests, but I made some sandwiches, and there is beer in the fridge."

"I could run and get a bottle of wine, if you prefer?" Nash directed his question to Rachel.

"Nothing will be open in town," I told him. "You'd have to drive almost to Granger."

"Beer and sandwiches sounds great to me," Rachel said. "I'm starving."

My wolf growled in dissatisfaction and I practically lunged for plates so I could put a sandwich in front of her. "Have a seat," I said as Nash opened the refrigerator and took out three bottles of craft beer he found on the door.

"You guys don't all drink the West Springs whiskey?" Rachel asked. Our town was known for the distillery, which was owned by Gib's family and provided jobs for most of the pack—anyone who wanted a job there, anyway.

"Nah," I said, sitting beside her at my small kitchen table. "Most of our whiskey gets exported. It's not special to the people who grew up here."

"We drink it in Montana," Nash said, popping open the beers with his thumb, even though they weren't twist-offs. Rachel's brows went up at his strength.

Nash and I would need to talk about when to share

our secret with Rachel. The sooner, the better, as far as my wolf was concerned, but I had to admit, I knew nothing about courting a human.

Nash might know a little more. I knew from Shelby that a whole rash of shifters in her pack had mated human females, and all of them fated mates, like ours. From a biological standpoint, I was interested in exploring the reason for that. It seemed a diversification of genes was necessary to ensure the shifter species. Heck, Landry and Wade had just mated Caitlyn, who was human.

I believed in evolution. Just as it had created the Two Marks breed to accommodate a lack of female shifters, now it seemed to be seeking to blend our DNA with humans. Almost always female humans to male shifters, though. I had yet to hear of a male human mating a female shifter.

I clinked bottles with Nash as our mate snatched up her sandwich and took a huge bite. We watched her eat for a moment. I was sure Nash had to be as fascinated by everything about her as I was.

"You ran from your old life, straight into our arms," Nash said, and picked up his sandwich.

Rachel gave a short laugh, and wiped her mouth with a napkin she grabbed from a holder in the center of the table. "That certainly wasn't the plan. But, yeah. I guess I did."

"What was so wrong with your ex?" I asked. She'd given me a little bit of information earlier, but it was time to get more details. "Not that I want to spend our time talking about him." I grimaced.

"I didn't love him," Rachel confessed, sounding like she felt guilty over it. "When I get married, I plan to marry for love, not because some guy wants an association with my family name to build his future political career."

Nash's brows shot up. "That was the deal?"

She nodded. "He wants to someday run for the Senate, and my family has political clout." She looked between the two of us. "My grandfather was governor in the '80s, and two of my uncles have been in local politics my entire life. Having me at Chester's side would've ensured name recognition and likeability," she explained.

I whistled. Rachel came from a prominent family. A well-known one. "I see. So you are the prize he needs to claim."

"Yes."

A muscle ticked in Nash's jaw. "He was going to use you," he growled, eyes flashing silver.

I shot him a warning glance, but his wolf was on

notice, ready to protect our mate, even though her ex was nowhere near us. "Did he hurt you?"

"No, never." Rachel's surprise couldn't be faked. "My parents wanted the connection, too. Their daughter being a senator's wife is a big deal for them. That's why they knew about the engagement party. They were all for the match. I wasn't."

It settled my wolf, everything she said, and Nash's eyes turned back to blue. Yeah, the sooner we marked and claimed our mate, the better. It seemed like Nash's wolf could be volatile when it came to Rachel. I didn't blame him, but a niggle of concern ran through me. I knew nothing about this guy—nothing of his history or temperament. Of course, Shelby trusted him, so that helped, but I'd only known her a few months.

Gibson knew Nash's pack alpha, and wouldn't have allowed Nash to leave with me to claim Rachel if he knew of any issues.

"Nash, what do you do?" she asked, then took another bite of sandwich.

"I run a construction company with my best friend," he said. "I guess I've always preferred partnership to working alone." He shot me a meaningful look. "Rand is going to be pissed when I don't return Monday."

"You aren't staying in West Springs for a while?"

Rachel asked in surprise. "Shelby said you might stick around, but—" She stopped and shook her head.

Nash nodded firmly. "I'm staying. Yeah. Definitely."

Rachel put her sandwich on her plate. "Wait... are you staying... for *me*?"

Nash sent another look my way, like he was looking for help, but I wasn't sure of the best way to play this, either.

"You're welcome to stay here at my place," I offered. It was the right thing to do. Once we'd marked our mate, we'd all be living together. We might need to get a bigger place, but we could figure that out. Hell, if Nash was in construction, maybe he could add on to my cabin. I'd bought a small house because I never expected to have a triad. "Both of you are," I added, looking at Rachel.

She gave a nervous laugh. Okay, we were probably both going too fast for a human.

"I have a place, but thank you," she said politely. "That's very nice of you."

"You'll stay tonight," Nash insisted, his eyes taking on a wolf-like glow again.

"Please," I interjected.

"All three of us?" She looked between us. "A slumber party?"

I managed to smile, as if the idea of her heading back to her apartment wasn't the most serious fucking topic in the world to my wolf. "Yeah, all three of us. I have a king bed, and we already know from the shower how much we like the Rachel sandwich."

Rachel blushed and shook her head, bringing her beer to her lips. "This is so crazy. I honestly can't believe it's happening."

"Oh, it's happening," Nash assured her with a wink. The guy could be charming, for sure. I doubted he'd ever had trouble landing a female in his life.

"My mother would faint dead if she ever found out," she admitted.

"That you'd been with two men at once?" I asked.

"Yes!" Rachel laughed and her cheeks turned pink. "She's the definition of propriety. All she ever worries about is how things look to the public. I mean, we are a political family, so appearances matter. If it ever got out that I'd been with two men at the same time..."

"I never kiss and tell," Nash said immediately, but his brows were down, and we exchanged a glance that spoke volumes.

Not only did we need to make our human mate fall in love with both of us, but we had to get her to agree to a lifetime. Requiring her to give up her family would be far too much to ask.

Yet it was workable. One of us could be her official husband and the other could remain in the background as a friend—at least to the outside, human world. It wasn't ideal to have to hide what we were, but it could be done. We had to hide we were shifters, anyway.

I realized Rachel was looking my way and I shook my head. "I never kiss and tell, either. You're safe with us, Rachel. You have my word."

"One hundred percent," Nash agreed. He'd finished his sandwich and polished off his beer. I drained mine as well.

Rachel looked between us. "You two... I don't understand how you could go from throwing punches at each other over me to sharing, just like that. This is so weird."

Nash cleared his throat. "I'm sorry about that. I'm embarrassed at how I acted. I just... I caught your sce —" He broke off when he saw my warning look. "I mean, I caught sight of you, and I sort of lost my mind for a minute. But then I was reminded I was in West Springs, where sharing females is a normal occurrence, and I realized I didn't have to be pig-headed about this. Especially considering Cord had found you first." His lips quirked in a grin to let her know he was teasing.

She rolled her eyes. "I'm not *finders-keepers.*"

He reached out and stroked a hand over her drying hair. "I know, beautiful. I'm willing to work for you." He glanced at me. "We both are."

"I'm not really, um, looking for something long term." Rachel flushed again. "I came to West Springs to figure out what I want to do with my life. I'm not really ready to jump into any kind of commitment."

Even though her words made sense, they hit me like a punch to the gut. My wolf wanted to howl, to rage at the delay. I had no doubt Nash was trying to remain calm too. We were *all* over commitment with her. One whiff, and there was no one else. Ever.

But Nash was right. We were willing to work for her. There was no other option.

"There's no pressure, Rachel," I assured her. "The only commitment I want from you is that you'll stay the night."

"And that you'll let us satisfy you one more time," Nash added with a grin. His gaze raked over her in just the t-shirt. "You tasted me. I am *dying* to taste you."

Rachel squirmed in her chair, and the scent of her arousal made both Nash's and my hands clench into fists. We sprang up from the table at the same time.

"I'll clean up," I said shortly, as if getting Rachel into my bed was a life-or-death emergency.

Nash seemed to understand perfectly. "I'll take care of our girl." He offered his hand to Rachel. As soon as she stood, he scooped her into his arms and carried her off to the bedroom. She squealed, then laughed.

Fuck the dishes. Rachel's scent still filled my nostrils, driving my wolf to a fresh frenzy. I stacked the plates in the sink, left the bottles on the table, and followed.

We had a lot to overcome to claim our mate, but making her scream in pleasure? I was certain we would succeed.

 ASH

AFTER FOOD AND TALKING, we'd all been ready for round two, and I'd gotten in that tight pussy of Rachel's. And yeah, the look on her face when I filled her up, I'd never forget. The way those snug walls rippled as she squirmed to get me to fit. Fuck. Making her scream my name was definitely my new mission in life. She'd practically passed out.

This morning, I'd have stayed in bed with Rachel between us. My job was in Montana, but Cord and Rachel had jobs here. She worked the lunch shift at the diner, but we'd woken her early with Cord's head between her thighs and my mouth on her nipples. We couldn't get enough of her. The need for me to take her rough, to bite her, was hard to control.

"Sore, beautiful?" I asked as she came into the kitchen. Cord had made coffee and I was leaning against the counter working through my first cup.

I wasn't exactly sure why, but the need for her pussy to be a little achy made my dick hard. Again. I wanted her to feel us while she was waiting tables.

She blushed but shook her head. "Those toys I had did the job of solving the whole painful-virgin-sex thing."

I went over to her, kissed her forehead, set my hand on the back of her neck. Her blue eyes flicked up to meet mine. Yeah, she felt the hint of possessiveness in the hold. "No more toys. You want to play, you've got two dicks to keep you happy."

She couldn't help but smile, which had been my intention. When she licked her lips, all I could think of was her mouth stretched wide around me. *Fuck.*

"I need to go home and change, then get to the diner."

My bag was at Shelby's. So was my truck. While Rachel was at work, Cord would have to take me to pick up both. I wouldn't be staying there. I'd be staying wherever Rachel was, and I had a feeling it was in Cord's bed.

Cord grabbed his keys. "Come on, we'll get you to the diner on time. Bessie's a ruthless boss."

The way Rachel laughed, I had to assume he was being sarcastic.

Cord's cell rang and he grabbed it from the counter. He glanced at the display, then at me. "Wade, what's up?"

I remembered Wade from Gibson's office. The IT guy who was going to look into my parents.

"Okay," he replied. "Sure. Yes. We're taking Rachel to the diner for her shift. How about we meet there in about thirty minutes?"

Wade must have found some news about my past. I'd forgotten all about it. A new mate and a virgin pussy had me distracted. But Rachel was going to be busy with the lunch shift, and I needed to learn the truth because what I'd known had been completely wrong. As Gibson and Cord had said, only pure Two Marks shifters scent matched. That meant my parents were from here.

Why had my grandparents kept it a secret? Why hadn't they told me I was from the Two Marks pack? I had so many questions and since I couldn't ask them, Wade was the guy with the answers.

"Everything okay?" Rachel asked as Cord led the way out to the garage.

"Fine, beautiful," I reassured. "We met Wade yesterday—"

"He's one of Caitlyn's men," Cord clarified. For a second, I panicked he was giving away that we were shifters, but then I remembered Rachel had met the woman and she had helped her understand our need for a threesome.

"Right. He wants to have lunch with us," I said. I wasn't going to lie to my mate. Never. But I didn't even know what the truth was at this point. All of it had to do with being a shifter, though, and we couldn't share that. Yet. Soon, we'd have to give her the full truth.

Thirty minutes later, Cord and I were tucked into a booth in Rachel's section of the diner. Wade showed up and I slid over so he could sit down. Rachel was busy with other tables, and without wolf hearing, she wouldn't overhear our conversation.

I pegged Wade to be in his early thirties. He had dark hair and was built as big as every shifter I knew. Knowing he was joining us, Rachel had brought three mugs for coffee and I filled his from the carafe she'd left for us.

"Thanks," he said, then took a sip without

doctoring it. He looked to me. "It wasn't too hard to find information on you or your parents."

I nodded, glad we weren't going to start with small talk. "When you have the missing piece of the puzzle —Two Marks—it's not all that hard."

He grinned. "Made my job easy." Then his smile fell away as he pulled a folded paper from his pocket and set it on the table. "You ready for this?"

My stomach churned and I put my mug down. "I'm guessing it's not good. Especially since my grandparents didn't tell me a thing before they died."

Cord glanced my way. I didn't know him all too well, but we were Rachel's mates together, which meant he had to know everything. There would be no secrets between us.

"Cathryn Taggart was from the Wolf Ranch pack."

I took a breath and relaxed my shoulders. "So my grandparents really are my grandparents. That's not a lie."

He shook his head. "Right. Ellen and Floyd only had one pup. Cathryn. Somehow —no one seems to remember how—she found her matched mates from the Two Marks pack. Harlan Fisher and Noble Mead."

I looked to Cord who said, "Never heard of them. I know one Fisher family, but they're too young."

"That's right," Wade confirmed. "I'd say those

Fishers might be cousins or something. The Meads moved to a Canadian pack when you were around one."

There was a lot Wade hadn't shared yet, only setting the foundation. My instinct told me none of it was good.

"What happened before then?" I asked.

He sighed. "I talked to my parents to get the story. They said Harlan wasn't a nice man. To put it mildly. He and Noble knew they were scent matches, but there was an age difference, and weren't friends prior to finding their mate."

"Meaning they had the connection but led completely separate lives," Cord clarified.

Wade nodded. "That's right. They met Cathryn—again, how that happened isn't known—and formed their triad. As all three were shifters, the connection was strong and from what I've found out, Cathryn was claimed right away."

"Okay," I said, not sure what the issue was.

Wade clenched his jaw. "Apparently, Harlan was rough."

"Rough with my mother?"

"With your mother and Noble," Wade confirmed.

I growled because that was not how shifter males

behaved. Females were cherished and protected. Never harmed.

"From what I gather, it's suspected Harlan wanted Cathryn for himself—he didn't want to share with Noble. When Jack West, the alpha at the time, refused to banish Harlan for what he'd done, they disappeared."

Cord made a funny sound and raised his hand. "I do remember this. I was really young when this happened, but the story of a bad match was talked about for years."

"That means that Harlan was a fucking asshole. Dangerous," I added.

Wade looked at his paper, avoiding my eyes. "I remember the story, too. Like Cord, I was little so the three shifters involved weren't *real*. Just a story. It got so that the names weren't even used. Just the bad shifter match. I'd forgotten about it and never made the connection to you. I wouldn't have unless I'd asked around."

Rachel came to the table, looked between the three of us. Her scent was sweet and strong and it soothed my riled wolf. I wanted to yank her onto my lap. No, I wanted to yank her onto my dick, sink into the pleasure I found in her body.

I couldn't. Not now.

I felt a stone rolling in the pit of my stomach. Here I'd been thinking I knew nothing about triads, but my biology would take over. My wolf would show me the way. But now I had to wonder if I should even attempt to be a part of Rachel's triad. My parents were the 'story' of the pack. The bad claiming that everyone talked about and remembered. I didn't think Wade's story was done, and suspected it was only going to get worse.

"I'm Wade," he said, introducing himself. He smiled and stood, tipping his cowboy hat.

Rachel smiled prettily up at him. I growled possessively, and Wade dropped back into his seat.

"You met his... Caitlyn yesterday," he added.

Rachel nodded, her eyes brightening with awareness as she made the connection. "Right. It's nice to meet you. You okay with coffee?"

She reached for the carafe and topped our mugs off, spilling some when she got to mine. "Whoops," she said, laughing at herself, taking a cloth from her apron and wiping up the mess.

He nodded. "Fine. I don't need a glass of water."

She looked to Cord, her mouth open. "You told him?"

"Told me what?" Wade asked.

Cord chuckled and grabbed her hand, kissing the knuckles. "I didn't tell him a thing."

She pursed her lips and switched topics. "Ready to order some food?"

We gave her our orders, then she headed for the kitchen. My wolf wasn't excited about that, and I stared at her ass as she went.

"Tell me about Harlan," I said, getting back on the subject once the swinging door closed behind her.

"Yeah. He was a loner," Wade continued. "Always had been. He worked as a mechanic—ran a shop in town, then he moved up into the hills and supported himself—barely—by repairing tractors, snowblowers, whatever had an engine, for shifters through the valley. Like a traveling vet."

"Go on," I said, knowing there was more.

Wade gave me a long, measured look that made the hairs on the back of my neck stand up. Then he laid it on me. "I'm guessing they sought protection from the alpha because of you."

The rock in my gut rolled over. "She was pregnant."

"That's my thought."

"They left. I guess they hid from Harlan in the Wolf Ranch pack with her parents. That's where you were born."

"They were that afraid of him?"

He nodded, grimly. "Apparently."

I glanced at Cord, who said, "I've never heard of a shifter behaving like this before. The instinct is to protect your mate and pup. Never to harm them."

"Why didn't he go to Wolf Ranch pack and bring them back?"

Wade shrugged. "He did."

I couldn't breathe. The air in the diner felt thick and hot. My hands were clenched into clammy fists, and I wanted to kill Harlan. "So, what happened?" I barely got the words out over my rusty windpipe.

Wade took a sip of his coffee. "Apparently there was an accident. Their car ran off the cliffs."

So at least that much was true. That was the story I'd been told growing up, that they'd died in a car accident.

Wade went on. "There was much speculation about them being run off the road, but local law enforcement couldn't prove anything. As I said, Jack West didn't banish Harlan from the pack, but word is he's been living alone a couple hours from here ever since. He's probably feral by now."

Banishment was a serious punishment for a wolf shifter, as we were pack animals. We craved and thrived in communities of our own kind. Lone wolves often went crazy living amongst humans or worse—totally on their own. But he hadn't been banished officially. He'd done it himself.

Wait. I caught on to something Wade had said. "You're telling me he's not dead?"

This guy... who'd probably killed my parents, who was an asshole, was alive?

Wade nodded.

"He needs to be put down," I growled.

"He's never been back here in all this time. Gibson knew nothing about you," Cord said to me. "Your parents, Noble and Cathryn, their plan worked. Harlan never learned about you."

And I'd never known about him. "My parents died to save me," I said, more to myself than Cord and Wade. "From him."

I pushed my coffee mug away, because the scent suddenly made me sick. My parents had died because of their own mate, or whatever he would be called. They'd been killed and their death had gone unavenged.

I supposed without proof, I couldn't very well avenge them either, but I was going to try. I was going to find this Harlan character and beat the truth out of him.

Rachel came our way carrying a tray covered in

dishes. My eyes widened as it tipped. Cord must have seen my reaction because his head whipped around and he stood quickly, taking it from her. He held it as she set down the plates, heavy with our lunch orders.

"Thanks," she said, going up on her tiptoes and giving Cord a kiss on the cheek when he handed her the empty tray.

She looked to me, then frowned. "What's wrong?"

Fuck. My jaw was clenched and I was seething with anger. And hurt. I couldn't explain any of it to Rachel. Hell, I could barely process it all, and I knew Wade wasn't done.

"I can't eat my fries without ketchup, beautiful," I managed to say.

Cord laughed. "I think we just figured out he gets hangry."

I wanted to tell him I didn't get angry when I was hungry, but he was helping me explain away my bad mood.

She grinned and went to grab the bottle and set it in front of me. She was sweet. Innocent. Untouched by all this. Except I had touched her the night before. Greedily. Aggressively.

Cord sat down and tucked into his meal. As if nothing was wrong.

When she was called away, I grabbed the ketchup

bottle and doused my fries in it even though I hated the stuff. "Anything else?" I grumbled, trying to deal with everything I'd just learned about myself.

Wade pulled a small photograph from his shirt pocket. "This."

I took it and stared. The photo was old, and of three people together. A dark-haired man had his arm slung around a woman's shoulders. They were clearly happy. Standing awkwardly beside them was another man... who looked exactly like me. Blond hair. Light eyes. The same angled jaw. Lips. Wide shoulders. Even close to the same age. It was as if I'd been computer-added to an old photo.

It all became clear then. I tossed the photo down on the table like it had burned me. "Fuck," I murmured.

Cord snagged it.

"I'm Harlan's kid," I choked out.

Wade nodded. "Cord's the expert on shifter DNA and gene study, but I'd say the fact that you look exactly like the guy is enough proof of that for me."

"Shit." Cord looked grim and nodded. He couldn't deny what he saw.

"Let me up," I said. My blood was boiling, and I felt like I was coming out of my skin.

Wade pushed to his feet and I slid out of the booth,

heading right for the door. Once out in the parking lot, I took a breath. All these years, I'd wondered.

No, that wasn't true. All the time growing up, I'd been content with my grandparents. They had been good people. Kind. Strong members of the pack. Excellent examples of what mates should be. That was one of the things that made me wish they were still alive. I was lost here with Cord and Rachel. I looked up at the cloudy sky. My grandparents had known I had two fathers, that my mother was matched and mated to two shifters. They'd known I had one of their genes, so why not tell me that?

Now I knew. I looked exactly like Harlan Fisher. The evil one. The one who was aggressive and angry. Uncontrolled. Oh fuck. Oh fates. It sounded way too fucking familiar.

ACHEL

So far, I had only dropped one plate and thankfully, it had been empty. Nothing with spaghetti sauce to mop up like the last time, only a quick sweep with a broom. Not only was I the usual bumbling waitress, but I was distracted.

Two hot guys did that to a girl. Two hot guys whom I'd had sex with not once, or twice, but three times—if having Cord eat me out as my alarm clock counted.

It *so* counted.

"You okay, hon?" Bessie asked, skirting behind me with a stack of laminated menus. I was at the counter, rolling silverware into napkins. The lunch rush was over and we only had one customer who was nursing a coffee and slice of pie.

"Sure," I replied.

"Your hand okay?"

I glanced down at the Band-Aid I'd put on this morning. I'd forgotten about the cut. "Doesn't hurt at all," I reassured her.

"I bet."

I looked up from what I was doing and saw her grin. Then she winked.

"I heard what happened at the barbecue. I don't know Nash, but Cord's a good man," she said.

I wasn't sure if she was trying to reassure me or what.

"They're both nice," I replied neutrally.

Nice and big. And bossy. And dominant. And possessive. And sexy. And... skilled.

I squirmed, my pussy awakened by the two, and eager for more. I had no idea what we were exactly, but I'd go with it. Take it one day at a time. It was easy to think that, but my heart was already involved. They'd had lunch with Wade. I'd seen Nash leave, Wade and Cord following soon after.

I missed them as soon as they were gone, which was weird, because I rarely thought about Chester. Not like this, wondering when I'd see them again. Craving the feel of their lips on mine, and other places.

Bessie laughed. "Nice." She leaned against the counter. "Honey, you got questions about all this? Two men being interested in you has got to be a little different."

My mouth fell open and I sat the silverware roll down. "You know about *that*?"

She set her hand on my shoulder and her shrewd gray eyes met mine. "You know I'm married to Pete."

I nodded, glancing through the passthrough window to the cook who whistled while he worked, and winked at me when I picked up my orders.

"I'm also married to Travis."

I frowned. "Who?"

"My other husband. He works our ranch. Rarely comes in."

I stared at her, dumbfounded. When Caitlyn and Shelby had said that the polyamory thing was a way of life here, I didn't think it would include my boss.

She squeezed my shoulder, then let her hand drop. "Don't look at me like that. I was young and pretty like you back in the day."

I blushed. "I'm sorry. I think it's great."

She grabbed a cloth and spray bottle and got to work spritzing and wiping down the menus. "That's good because both Cord and Nash are interested in you."

"Yeah, I figured it out."

"And?"

She kept her eyes on her work so I went back to mine. "And?" I repeated.

"Got questions?"

I shrugged. "I like them. A lot. Both of them. I wouldn't know how to pick one if I had to."

"That's good. You told me you ran away from home because of a pushy boyfriend."

"You make me sound like a six-year-old," I muttered, except I had run away.

"If a man bothers you enough to leave the state, then he isn't the guy for you."

I didn't say anything, only rolled more silverware into napkins and stacked them in a container.

"There's a difference between pushy and how Cord and Nash feel for you."

I turned and glanced her way.

"I'd say they're... dominant. I don't like that word... *pushy*. Those two will never do anything you don't want. Your needs come first, hon, with them. Doesn't sound like the ex felt that way."

I was quiet as I mentally compared. Cord and Nash

were nothing like Chester, not in any way. "I wouldn't call Cord and Nash *pushy*. They're... eager."

"They're not golden retrievers," she countered.

"Rottweilers," I countered. Loyal. Protective. Gentle. But ruthless if needed. I'd seen them fight.

"You got it." The bell over the door jingled and Bessie called, "Sit anywhere you—"

"I finally found you."

My head whipped up at that voice. My heart leapt into my throat, and I stared at Chester. Panicked. Wide eyed.

"Chester," I whispered. "What are you doing here?"

He wore tan slacks and a crisp button up. His hair was meticulously styled. I saw the sheen on his nails, meaning he'd had a manicure recently. Had his tan always looked so fake? After being with Cord and Nash, Chester seemed so... unmanly.

His shoulders stiffened. "I'm here for you, of course. Why else would I be in this Godforsaken town? Wyoming, babe?" He looked around as if he was slumming.

Bessie made a funny sound, then headed for the kitchen.

I was thankful for the counter between us. "I like it here." I tipped my chin up, defending the place.

He took a step closer, set his hands on the worn laminate. "That's great. I'm glad you've had your fun. It's time to come home. Your mother's been sick with worry."

I was sure, with one of her migraines, which only gave her the excuse to drink more wine and get a refill on her pain pills.

"I'll call her."

"You'll ride with me, and your father will have someone return your car."

I shook my head. "No. I'm staying here."

He tsked me. "We're engaged. I told everyone you were overcome with emotion after you fled the party. They understood, the surprise was so great."

He pulled a small black box from his pocket, flipped the lid open and pulled out a huge diamond. "You didn't stay around for this."

As if receiving a marquise cut diamond was going to change my mind. It was big and, while beautiful, completely not me.

I looked him in the eye. "We're not engaged, Chester. I said no."

"The photographer comes on Tuesday. They're holding a spot in the paper for the announcement."

I ran a hand over my hair, frustrated. This was why

I'd left. But I wasn't going to keep on running. It was time to put a stop to all this.

The diner door swung open and in stalked Cord and Nash. I had no idea where they'd been, but it had to have been close by. Bessie must have called them from the kitchen.

The relief that flooded through me made me smile. My heart beat for them. I realized it now, having my old life and my new life side by side.

Nash approached. "You okay, beautiful?"

Chester turned to look at Nash and had to tilt his chin up to meet his gaze. "Who the hell are you?"

Nash's jaw clenched and his shoulders went back. I thought of the fight he had with Cord the day before, and didn't want that now. It was one thing to break a dish or two, but I didn't want a fight in Bessie's diner because of me.

I didn't think, only blurted the first thing that came to mind. The only thing that would put an end to Chester's quest. "He's my husband."

Chester stilled. Nash froze. Cord stayed in the background, but close enough to get to Chester if needed. He set his thumbs in his front pockets, and the corner of his mouth twitched.

Out of the corner of my eye, I saw Bessie come out of the kitchen and then she stood beside me.

"Husband?" Chester sputtered. "Impossible." His face flushed and a vein popped out in his temple. "This... cowboy?" He looked Nash over as if he were wondering where he'd been spawned.

I saw the brawny man with the Stetson, the focused intensity, and thought of his mad skills in the sack. Nash was *all* cowboy.

A lie would get Chester to go back to California and out of my life. Except I may have exaggerated what was between me, Nash and Cord. We'd had one night. I was sure neither of them expected my words to be real. I only needed Chester to leave, and then it wouldn't matter. We'd laugh it off.

"Yes," I said. "Married to this cowboy."

"You've been gone three weeks, and you got married?" he sputtered.

I had been brought up to fake it as long as I kept a smile on my face. I plastered one on right now and relied on my upbringing to get me through this. "When it's love at first sight, why wait?"

Nash turned his gaze away from Chester as if he wasn't worth any more of his time, and studied me. Not like Chester had when he'd first come in, disgusted to see me in my cheap diner t-shirt and jeans. My hair, while neat, was pulled back in a simple ponytail. I had on a hint of makeup, but not my usual 'full face' I'd been expected to put on before leaving the house ever since ninth grade.

"That's right, beautiful," Nash agreed.

My smile shifted. Less fake. Relief coursed through my veins that he'd play along.

"I don't believe you," Chester said and he wiped his mouth with the back of his hand. "You wouldn't give up your life for *him*."

"Yes, I would." I said it without thinking. I would. I'd walked away, and hadn't missed a second of the old Rachel. I didn't know who the new Rachel was exactly, but I liked the idea of Nash being in her life. Marrying him was pushing it, but it was the first thing I thought of. If it got Chester gone, then that was all that mattered.

I'd apologize to Nash for the lie and thank him for backing me. Later.

"Just this morning, you were singing my praises," Nash said, all calm and cool. "Loudly." He winked.

Chester's hands clenched.

Nash was intentionally messing with Chester, and having fun doing it.

"He's just after your inheritance!" Chester boomed.

Nash growled and came closer. Cord took a step forward, his eyes catching the light in a weird way.

Suddenly, things became very, very clear. Chester

didn't just want my family name for his political career. He was relying on the inheritance from my grandfather for his campaign. The one I could access the moment I married. Grandpa had been sexist that way. He thought a woman needed a man to manage her money. Just like my parents never considered me able to run for political office, only a husband of mine.

"He doesn't know about the inheritance," I said quietly. "But clearly it's at the forefront of *your* mind."

Chester seemed to recover then, pulling himself together. "Of course it's at the forefront of my mind. I don't want to see you taken advantage of, Rach. And this whole thing reeks of manipulation."

I let out a soft scoff and looked away. I'd never been rude to Chester before. I didn't think we'd ever even had a fight. That showed how little we really cared about each other. But I was seeing him in a different light right now, and what I'd seen couldn't be unseen. Chester was the one who'd been manipulating me. Of course, I'd known that, but it felt far more clear and intentional now. Not like two people who were going through life without being sure of what they wanted, which is how I'd seen us, but like a predator and his quarry.

I was Chester's meal ticket and he didn't want to give me up. I guessed I'd known that on a subconscious level, or I wouldn't have claimed I was married to Nash. The only true way to make Chester go away.

Cord remained quiet and watchful, ready to step in, but he couldn't get involved. It was one thing for people in West Springs to accept two men with one woman, but Chester sure as hell wouldn't.

"You aren't wearing a ring," Chester snapped.

Oh shit.

"Like that one there?" Nash pointed to the engagement ring on the counter. "Nah. It'd get caught in my hair when you tugged it, beautiful. I know how much you like to do that."

"You've slept with him?" Chester shouted.

I wasn't sure if I should feel sorry for the man at the end of the counter who'd come in for coffee and pie, or if he was enjoying his front row seat to my insanity.

"I am married to him," I replied.

"Prove it," Chester snapped.

"I didn't save the bed sheets," Nash countered.

I couldn't help but blush. I had been a virgin the night before, but Nash was being a little too bold.

"That you're married," Chester seethed. "I want to see the marriage license."

Oh shit. My gaze flicked to Nash.

Cord looked to Bessie. I saw her give him a nod,

like they'd had a silent conversation. She went back to the kitchen.

"I was a witness," Cord improvised. "It happened."

Chester finally gave Cord a once over. "Who the fuck are you?"

I'd never heard him swear before, a sure sign he was angry and not trying to stay in his political facade.

"Cord McCaffrey, town doctor."

"I don't care if you're the Pope. Show me a marriage license or I'm not fucking leaving town."

Cord looked to Nash. I stayed silent because I couldn't think of a thing to say. A lie was one thing, but a marriage license? I didn't have a magic wand. God, what a mess! How could I talk myself out of this one?

"We want you to leave town because you're clearly upsetting Rachel, so why don't we head down to the courthouse and get you a copy?" Cord spoke. "I doubt you have the license on you, do you, Nash?"

Nash patted his body as if he were searching for it. "Nope."

Was Cord serious? The *courthouse*? I wasn't sure if I wanted to throw up or run away again.

Chester glanced between us. "Fine. Once I find out this wedding never happened, you're coming with me."

"I'm not going with you, no matter what, Chester," I replied.

"We'll see about that."

Nash moved and loomed over Chester. "Don't threaten my wife, because I'm the one you'll have to deal with."

Chester took a step back and paled.

Keeping his eyes on Chester, Nash held out his hand. "Come 'ere, beautiful."

Bessie came out of the back, and I caught her eye as I went around the counter. "Go with Nash, hon. Everything's gonna be all right."

I wasn't so sure, but I couldn't think of a thing to say to fix this mess I'd put us all in.

I only wanted Chester to go away. Now I was afraid Nash would beat him up. That Bessie's diner would be destroyed. That good people would get hurt because of my stupidity.

What must Cord and Nash be thinking right now? They had to hate me for getting them into this mess.

I took Nash's hand and he tugged me close, kissing the top of my head.

Chester glared.

"You want proof," Cord said. "It's this way. Just down the block."

Cord turned and left the diner, expecting Chester to follow.

He did.

So did Nash and I. He didn't let go of my hand the entire way to the courthouse at the end of the block.

Cord led us into the old brick building and down a hall to the right. He went to a door smartly painted with *Clerk and Recorder* across the glass, and opened it.

He held it for Chester, and gave me a wink behind Chester's back.

The office we entered was small. There were only two desks in front of a window overlooking the central town square. A woman stood. I guessed her to be in her mid-fifties, with graying hair. She wore an orange sweater and a huge smile.

"There you two are," she said, looking to me and Nash. "I wondered when you would come back. You left here in such a hurry the other day, you didn't even sign the paperwork." She waggled her eyebrows at me.

When I realized my mouth was hanging open, I snapped it shut.

All praises to the workings of a small town. Bessie must have done this, called this woman to have her in on the lie. I couldn't believe it.

She set a piece of paper on her desk and waved a pen at us. Nash and I stepped forward. It was a marriage license with our full names on it, and dated three days earlier. The officiant spot was signed, and so was the witness line. She must have hustled to get this pulled together as we walked from the diner.

Nash took the pen and signed beneath the line for the groom, then handed it to me.

"Now just a minute." Chester tried to snatch the pen from me.

Nash blocked his reach with a slice of his hand and Chester pulled it back, shaking it like he'd cracked his wrist. Nash held his gaze with blazing challenge.

Chester ground his teeth, but didn't speak again.

I signed my name on the spot for the bride.

What was I signing? It had to be fake. This woman was in on whatever was going on. I'd just wanted Chester to believe that Nash and I were married, then drive off in a spray of gravel. But now I was in the county courthouse, signing a marriage license?

"I chased after them, but Nash had Rachel tossed over his shoulder. It wasn't like I was going to stop the lovebirds for a piece of paper," Cord added as we finished.

The woman laughed. "They were so cute," she agreed.

What?

"They're actually married?" Chester asked, snatching up the paper and reading it.

"They are. Is there a problem?" the woman asked, her smile slipping before she gave him a haughty look my mother would be proud of.

Chester spun on his penny loafer's heel and glared at me. He waved a finger in my face. I'd never seen him angry like this before. Not once in all the years we were *together* had he been anything but mild. I could see now, it had all been an act. This was the real Chester. I couldn't understand why he was so angry. We didn't make out. We definitely didn't have sex. There were other women out there who would love to be his arm candy. Why come all the way to Wyoming after me?

I could see his mind working. He quickly masked his anger again. "You've had a nervous breakdown," he counseled me, like he was preparing a story for the court. "This can be annulled."

Oh, crap. I could see where he was going with this. He was preparing his legal case. The one that ensured he still got to marry me and use my inheritance.

"I will talk to your father, and we'll take care of this," he added.

I drew myself up. "It's done. I didn't have a breakdown. I'm perfectly sane and of sound mind. I will talk to my father, myself. Now *go*."

"This isn't over, Rachel."

I opened my mouth to answer, but Nash did it for me. "It is," he snapped. "I don't know who the fuck you are or why you think you're anything to my wife. There's nothing between the two of you. She made it clear, and now I'm telling you. Get the fuck out of her life."

 ORD

HOLY SHIT. There was a lot to absorb today. When I'd dreamed of having a scent match and a mate, I'd never pictured this. First, we found out from Wade that Nash was the son of an abusive and quite possibly murderous wolf. Now Rachel had just married the guy.

Not that I objected. Locking her down in this relationship was our goal, so having the paper ticket humans required to prove a union was a win, even if I wasn't the husband named on said paper.

When Rachel blurted out she and Nash were

married, I'd lost my shit. That had been a bad move, but my wolf had been pleased. It was our number one priority as shifters to protect our mates and get rid of any threats. We couldn't kill a human and bury him in the woods, no matter how much my wolf wanted to do that with Chester. Marriage was what the fucker wanted with Rachel. Having her legally bound to someone else instead solved that problem.

Wolf happy.

But it didn't solve any of our actual problems. She'd tossed those words out as a lie. She hadn't meant them. So we couldn't tell her about us being shifters, and we couldn't claim her.

Nash was a wild card, and now legally bound to her. Would I have to protect our mate from her other match just as Noble had done for Nash's mother?

Fuck.

We had to convince her to want to be married and bound to both of us. For real. To let us mark her and claim her for life. I didn't think either of us were going to go moon mad too soon, but I didn't know of any match based on a lie. And secrets. And a dark history.

As soon as Chester walked out, we drew Rachel into a three-way hug. When I felt her body trembling, a low growl formed in my throat. I was ready to chase Chester down and bury him like I'd imagined.

"Are you okay, beautiful? He's gone."

We released her, and stood back.

"I'm fine. I'm just *pissed off*," she said, but tears formed in her eyes. "Here I thought all this time I was just confused. I wanted to please everyone and make things work with Chester, the way they were supposed to. I thought I was the asshole for not wanting such a perfect guy."

This time, it was Nash who growled.

"He's *not* a perfect guy. Far from it. He just wanted my money!" She sounded so offended as she flung her arms in the air.

No way that man was in love with her. His intentions were obvious, and far from pure.

"I mean, I think I knew it on some level. I thought we were mutually using each other. I thought I was okay with that. An easy, perfect-on-paper match, that sort of thing. We had the right families, the right status, a shared history. All that stupid high-society political stuff. But he was straight up using me for his own gain. He didn't care about me at all!"

Tears streamed down her cheeks and she wiped them away.

Fuck, tears. Her cheeks were flushed and she paced the small space. Norma, the county clerk, watched quietly. I wasn't sure how much Bessie had told her to get the license made in time. I was thankful Bessie and I had thought the same thing, and that Norma was all for getting dumbass humans to leave town.

Norma went over and put an arm around Rachel's slim shoulders. "Come on, sweetheart. Let's go to the ladies' room and get you cleaned up. That guy isn't worth your tears. You've got these two right here."

Rachel turned her teary eyes to me, then Nash, and let Norma lead her out of the office and down the hall.

While Rachel couldn't hear me from the restroom, I stepped close to Nash. "Well, shit," I murmured.

He took off his hat, ran his free hand through his hair. "I'm sorry, man. It should have been you. I'm—I don't know if I'm cut out for this Two Marks thing. And now I'm the one fucking married to her. While I don't give a shit about human marriages, I at least figured it would be legit."

"It's legit," I said, looking at the paper lying on the desk. "But still a lie. She didn't do it because she wanted you for the rest of her life."

"And she shouldn't," he said, his eyes filled with a mix of bleakness and anger. "You heard what Wade said about Harlan. There's no question that I've got his

DNA. I'm not suited for a triad. I'm way too aggressive. Rough. I wanted to rip her ex apart."

I shook my head. "Yeah, but not like that asshole Harlan. It could just be your wolf, eager now that you've found your mate."

He gave me a look that questioned my intelligence. "Maybe Harlan blamed it on his wolf too." He sighed. "Why couldn't she have married you?"

I wondered that also. "She didn't. We can't change the paperwork now. I doubt that fucker's done with Rachel, so she has to stay protected."

His spine stiffened. "I won't hurt her. I'm telling you that. I don't *want* to. But if you see me doing any shit that would put her in danger, you put me down. Or get an enforcer to do it. Ben, or my pack member, Clint."

His pale eyes met mine. He was fierce in this. Intent. This was where the true Nash showed through. His integrity. I didn't know him at all, but I trusted him now. Knew he was the scent match I'd always hoped to have.

"Done."

He nodded, clearly relieved.

"Rachel's going to be back in a minute and we need to get our shit together. Nothing's changed," I continued. "Except you might question being married to her, but it's the way it has to be. To protect her. Chester wants her money and her family's political standing, whatever the fuck that is."

"We need to get Wade to look into him," Nash said.

"Agreed. He can't touch it, though, if she's married to you. We want to keep her safe, and this is one way to do it."

"Fine," he said, gritting his teeth. "You know what you need to do."

Another reminder for me to watch him.

"And you need to smile. Be happy you got roped into a fake marriage. Gibson told us to get our marks on her. We need to make that paper mean something. Mean *everything*."

He nodded, set his hat back on his head. Resolute. "That's how we make it all happen. Turn it from fake to fan-fucking-tastic."

I couldn't help but smile. Nash was back in the game.

Rachel and Norma came through the door. Rachel looked at us tentatively, but her eyes were dry and a smile was on her face. "I'm so sorry, Nash. I didn't think my lie would turn into all this."

Nash went over to her, leaned down, and kissed her sweetly. "There's nothing for you to be sorry for, beautiful. That douche canoe needed to be sent back to California. I'm glad you turned to me to help."

"But marrying you?"

He laughed. "There are worse things for you than being stuck married to a gorgeous, sexy cowboy like me."

She stepped back and poked him in the ribs. That got a smile out of both of them.

"Neither of us are like Chester," I said, stating the obvious. "We'd want you if you were penniless and grew up in a gutter. You can count on that. We have more than enough to provide for you in every way."

A sniff came from behind the desk, and I turned to see Norma wiping an eye. "It's my turn to be a watering can now. Fated matings always make me cry," she explained.

I gave a little shake of my head to impart that Rachel didn't know what that meant, and she looked down and busied herself stacking papers.

"Thank you for getting that license together, Norma. You saved the day," I said.

"You did," Rachel breathed, turning to face Norma.

"I just live for a good love story, and it sounds to me like you've got one with these two men."

Rachel glanced up at both of us with... hope in her eyes.

Nash reached over and shook Norma's hand. "Thank you for your help, ma'am."

Norma beamed at the three of us. "You three go enjoy each other. And leave that license here for me to file!"

"But we're not really married now, are we?" Rachel asked, wide eyed. "Can't you throw it out? I mean, Chester's gone."

"You heard the guy," Nash said, repeating the words we'd discussed. "He's not done here. We have to file it."

Rachel bit her lip and considered. "You're right. I mean, you're okay with this, Nash? If he finds out things weren't done legally, he'll cause trouble. Did you hear how he was already laying the seeds to get me declared incompetent or something?"

"I heard it," I said grimly. Chester was a real piece of work, that was for sure. Probably dangerous. Not physically, but legally.

The marriage license might be a human binding document, but Rachel had the entire Two Marks pack behind her. Since Nash was in the Wolf Ranch pack, she had them on her side as well. Chester had no idea how big a fight he had on his hands.

"Hmm, am I okay being married to the beautiful female who has utterly captivated my mind, body and soul? Let me think about it for a minute..." Nash mused, tapping his chin. Not a hint of Harlan was in his words or the heated looks he sent our mate's way.

Rachel visibly relaxed for the first time since Chester had shown up, and a slow smile spread across her lovely face.

"Yeah, I think I'm good." Nash tipped his cowboy hat. "Come here. Don't I get to kiss my bride?"

Rachel leaned into him and he wrapped an arm around her waist and pulled her in for a long, slow kiss.

Norma sighed.

I cleared my throat. I wasn't jealous—it just didn't happen with scent matches. But that didn't mean I didn't want a little sweetness for myself. "Do I get one, too?"

Rachel gasped, like she'd hurt my feelings. "Cord!" She whirled to face me, putting both her palms on my chest. "I'm so sorry. Are you upset that I married Nash? I mean—"

I stopped her with my mouth on hers, swallowing her explanation and apology with a kiss I hoped said she was everything to me. After a moment, she relaxed and moaned into the kiss. When we finally pulled apart, her gaze was unfocused and her cheeks were flushed.

"You guys are so amazing," she said. "I don't even understand it. How is it possible that you could be so perfect?"

"We're just perfect matches," I told her, because it was scientific fact.

She frowned. "But how are you so sure about me? It can't be love at first sight for both of you. Does that even happen in real life?"

"Oh, it happens," Norma interjected, still gleefully listening in on our exchange. "Love at first sight, love at first scent..."

I gave her a warning look, and she shot me a mischievous smile. Well, who could blame her? Fated matches were not the norm, and exceedingly important to the survival of our pack's breed. It made sense that the entire town would be rooting for me to mark my mate, whether they knew Rachel and Nash or not. Especially since they all knew I hadn't found my scent match, or my mate, until the day before.

I was glad there wasn't too much prejudice against matches with humans in these parts.

But Rachel didn't experience love at first scent. Humans didn't understand the biology behind a mating. I knew she sensed our connection, but in her human reality, it took time and shared experiences to fall in love. We needed to fast track that with her so we could lock her into our triad.

The trouble was, after what we learned this morning about Nash's parentage, I wasn't so sure myself that this could all work out.

Maybe I should be worried that Rachel just legally married my scent match, considering I didn't know the guy, and his genes were tainted with violence and a history of failed mating.

"I don't know about you, but I'm ready to consummate this marriage." Nash flashed me a smile.

"I think you already did that, big guy," Rachel said with laughter in her voice.

"We haven't consummated the threesome yet," I said, even though it was probably too soon. Rachel had been a virgin yesterday. She probably wasn't ready for double penetration yet.

But something about the uncertainty over Nash made it feel important. Like I didn't just need to mark and claim my mate, but I had to lock him in as well. I wanted to banish the niggling fear I had over trusting him.

If we wanted Rachel, we needed to be sure of each other.

So no better time than the present to push things forward another step.

 ACHEL

ON THE DRIVE to Cord's house, I called my parents with my new cell. I hadn't talked to them since I fled the country club. Hadn't told them where I was going. They'd probably left tons of messages on my old cell, which I never listened to. While they'd been in on the engagement party, I knew they loved me. Wanted what was best, even if it was what *they* thought it should be. It was my fault, too. I'd enabled them for a long time, going along with Chester and our *dating*. I should have dumped him years ago. Should have told my parents more forcefully how unhappy I was with him.

I'd done that at the surprise party, that was for sure. Things were different now. I was married.

I needed to talk to my dad, specifically. My mom was going to freak out about my supposed marriage, but it was Chester's connection with my dad that worried me. If he started pushing this 'break-down' story, then I was going to have even more trouble than I imagined with being left alone to live my life.

I thought of how Chester saw me here in West Springs. I worked in a diner. I'd never had a job in my life. I had dated and married a cowboy. Nash wore snug Wranglers and a Stetson. Sturdy leather work boots, not penny loafers. It was a surprise for me too. But I was okay with it. I liked working. I liked snug jeans. I liked Nash. I liked how living in West Springs made me feel. Like I was living my own life.

To Chester, I'd gone insane.

To me, maybe I'd actually fled insanity and found the real me.

"Dad?"

"Rachel!" he boomed. "Oh my God, sweetheart, is it true? What in the hell is going on?"

I shrank a bit in the passenger seat of Cord's SUV and held the phone away from my ear.

Cord frowned, shooting me a concerned look. Something about his gruff concern straightened my backbone. I had a right to find my own way in the world. Letting the people close to me manage my life was what got me into this mess.

"Is what true?" I asked.

"Have you completely lost it?" His voice was loud enough I didn't have to put my phone to my ear. I was sure they guys could hear. "You ran away from your own engagement party and married a cowboy in Wyoming?"

Chester had gone and tattled to my parents. It had taken less than thirty minutes. Unbelievable!

"Dad, you're yelling," I said, trying to remain calm. "I'm fine. Happy. Safe. Call me back when you're ready to listen." I ended the call, then clapped a hand over my mouth, shocked at my own audacity. I'd never once talked back to either of my parents. I'd gone along with their wishes. Clearly, for far too long.

"Good for you," Nash encouraged, setting his hand on my thigh and giving it a gentle squeeze. Cord was driving, I was in the middle—where they seemed to like me—and Nash on my right.

The phone immediately rang. I gave it a couple rings before I picked up the call. *"Rachel."* My dad sounded worried now. "Are you on drugs?"

I shook my head and ended the call again. "He just

asked if I was on drugs," I said in shocked disbelief. Chester really had already done a number on him.

The phone rang again, and this time I took charge. "Dad, if you're going to insult me or my mental capacities, we're not having this conversation. Are you ready to listen?"

He made a frustrated sound in his throat, and then choked out, "Okay."

I took a deep breath. I'd been rehearsing this speech in my head for weeks, but hadn't really gotten it right yet. "I'm not marrying Chester. I should have figured that out sooner, but I guess I had a hard time letting people down. You and Mom included. In my defense, I've been saying I wasn't ready or sure about marriage to him for years now, and every time I did, you or Mom told me why it would be perfect."

My dad made a noncommittal sound.

"I have to say that springing an engagement party on me as a surprise was a bad move. Putting me on the spot didn't make me cave, it made me leave the state. So, you only have yourselves to thank for my current address."

My dad let out a dry laugh. Hearing it relieved me.

"I'm sorry I haven't been in touch. It was disrespectful. I needed some time without any pressure. I just wasn't ready to talk to anyone yet. I'm sure you and Mom were worried, so I apologize for that."

"Well, are you sure you're safe? What is this business about marrying a cowboy? I can get that wedding annulled and have you back here in twenty-four hours."

He loved me. He did. But he was trying to save me. I needed to save myself. Live with my decisions, face the consequences.

I'd been the one who'd lied and said Nash was my husband. I had to deal with that. But with Nash—and Cord—I owed it to them to stick around. Plus, I *wanted* to stay. To see what this was between us. Not that I could share that with my father.

"Yes, I'm fine. Nash is a good man."

Nash stiffened beside me and I set my hand on top of his.

"You barely know him."

"I know good when I see it," I murmured, recognizing the truth in the words. I'd never felt anything but *right* with these two men.

Nash made a funny sound, and I looked up and met his blue eyes.

I saw the heat. Felt it.

"Look, Dad. I've got to go. I know Chester told you things, but it's over with him."

"That man is angry. He called and acted insane. I've never heard him like that."

"I know I embarrassed him at the party, but he embarrassed me too. Then he shows up here, and is furious I moved on."

"You *married* a guy. I wouldn't call that simply moving on."

I was tempted to tell my dad I married Nash to send Chester the message that my inheritance was off the table, but something in me didn't want to say that things with Nash were a farce. Maybe I didn't want them to be a farce.

I sighed. "You're right. Either way, Chester has no say. Move on, marry, move to Mars. It's my decision. I'm going to say it again so it's clear for you. I'm not in love with Chester. I don't even *like* him right now. I am not going to marry him or date him. It's over."

"I hear you."

I nodded, even though he couldn't see me. "Good. I'll call you again soon, and we'll talk more."

14

 ASH

CORD LED Rachel into his house. While my wolf didn't understand what a marriage license meant, it preened with satisfaction because it somehow knew we were connected. It also prowled because our mate was with us. Unclaimed. Her sweet scent was like a drug. I needed it in my nostrils, on my skin. Coating my dick. I wanted her flavor on my tongue. And I wanted my mark on her. I knew many left it on the place where the shoulder and neck met.

For some reason, I wanted to see mine on the delicate skin on the inside of her thigh. I'd be careful of her artery there, but knowing every time I settled in to lick and eat her pussy, I'd see my claim...

My dick hardened thinking about it. My mouth watered, craving her taste.

"Now what?" Rachel asked, suddenly shy. She looked everywhere but at me.

Was she doubting the marriage? Me?

"Now, we take you again," Cord said, reaching up to carefully slide her hair tie from her ponytail.

"Because I married Nash?" she asked.

I glanced at Cord and from the dark look in his eyes, I knew he was waiting for me to join in.

"No," he said. "Because I've been thinking about it ever since we left the house this morning."

He tugged the hem of her diner t-shirt up, and Rachel raised her arms.

She wore a different bra today. It was black and lacy but had straps that did absolutely nothing except make my dick punch against my jeans. While it seemed to have those underwire things, the lace didn't even cover the bottom curve of her tits.

"Fuck me," I breathed, staring. "You've had that on all day?"

Cord growled. "Hell, we'd have never left the house."

I moved closer, unable to resist touching her. I ran a finger over the lace and watched her nipple harden beneath the delicate fabric. Those lush mounds jiggled with the way she was panting.

"Do the panties match?" Cord asked. His gaze tipped down as he took in his fill of her body.

"Always. They always have to match," she said, and I remembered she'd told us this before.

Cord worked the button on her jeans, then knelt down to slide them off her legs. He remained on his knees before her once he had her stripped down to that sexy set she had on.

I plucked at one of those useless but sexy-as-fuck straps on her bra. Gave it a little tug. It ripped at the top, and I held it in my fingers. "Oops," I said, then let it drop so it dangled. The little bit that was broken was fucking killing me. As if she was already slightly mussed.

"You will not rip all my pretty things," she scolded, although when it came out in such a breathy way, the sting of it was lessened. Especially since Cord's hands were caressing her legs from ankle to hip.

"I'm not sure if I can help it," I admitted. Her gaze lifted to meet mine. "I need you so badly. I'm going to be rough."

There, I had told her. I'd warned her. If I could rip

sexy lingerie with a little twist of my fingers, I could hurt her.

"I like it rough," she countered, tipping her chin up.

My wolf practically howled. "You don't know what you're saying."

"Because I was a virgin until yesterday? I told you. I never had a dick in me. That's it. It doesn't mean I'm clueless. I like it rough. With both of you. And if you can't help ruining my lingerie, then take it off."

Cord huffed out a laugh. "My pleasure, beautiful." His fingers hooked into the strappy sides of her panties and slid them down. When they were pooled around her ankles, she lifted one foot, then the other, and he flicked the black lace away. "Look at this pretty pussy. It belongs to me and Nash, doesn't it?"

I watched as he leaned in, licked her.

She gasped and instinctively stepped wide.

Carefully, I unhooked her bra, let it slide down, and snagged it to drop it to the floor and not on Cord's head.

She gasped and settled her hands into Cord's dark hair. Watching our mate, naked and getting eaten out was sweet, gorgeous torture. I undid my jeans, slid down the zipper to give my dick some room.

"Nash, you need a taste of this." Grasping her hips, Cord turned her so she faced away from me. He shifted so he was eating her out again.

I stared at that pert ass and knew what he was offering. I settled on my knees so she had her mates front and back, and I placed my hands on those perfect globes. Parting them.

I'd never had anal sex before. I'd thought it was fucking hot, but had never gotten there. Since sex had always been to burn off excess energy and restless need after a full moon run, it had been nature driving me. My baser needs to fuck had made it vanilla.

Rough, wild, vanilla.

I hadn't even spanked a female's ass. It had never come up, those extra... desires.

I'd pushed them down, just like my thoughts that something had been missing in a male/female shifter pairing.

Not only had a second male been missing, but so had ass play. I craved to see my handprint on that pale flesh, so I gave Rachel a little spank. She gasped and bucked into Cord's mouth. The gasp switched to a moan, so I did it again.

"Fuck, that made her drip. Taste," Cord growled.

I didn't need to be told again. Tipping her forward

slightly, I got my mouth on that pussy from behind. Licked up all that need. Got her flavor on my tongue, that sticky sweetness on my chin.

"Oh!" she cried. Yeah, she'd never thought about being with two guys either.

But she liked it. Her sounds, the way her pussy all but soaked my face, were proof.

Fuck.

Coating my finger in her honey, I slid it into her pussy as I soon would my dick, but didn't linger. I used that wetness to coat her back entrance, the place we'd take her. Soon. For now, I'd play. Give in to the desires that drove me.

When I circled that puckered hole, she startled.

"Shh, beautiful. Let Nash play. He's going to make it so good for you. Being with the two of us means you're going to have *all* your needs fulfilled. Even ones you didn't even know you had," Cord said.

I collected a little more of her nectar and played some more. Feeling her resistance, I was careful, but I was getting my finger in there.

"Like that?" I asked, staring up at her past her handprint-marked ass.

She looked over her shoulder at me. Her cheeks were flushed, eyes glazed. There was a hint of embarrassment, but she bit her lip and nodded.

"Such a good girl. Nothing's wrong with this," Cord told her. Then he put his mouth back on her clit and began to work her. I could feel his finger, then two, inside her pussy when she finally flowered open, and I breached her to the knuckle.

She clamped down, just as I imagined she would with my dick. Eventually.

It didn't take long. With her clit being licked and her pussy and ass finger fucked, she came on a scream. Her body shook and her hand dropped, her fingers of one hand trying to get purchase on my short hair, and she also grabbed at Cord's.

Cord pulled back when she calmed, kissed her mound, then wiped his mouth with the back of his hand. I carefully removed my finger.

I stood, scooped her up into my arms and carried her to Cord's bed.

"Liked having both of us work you like that?"

She was up on her knees, her pert nipples pointing at me. Her lower lips were pouty and swollen and even from a few feet away, I saw her clit was hard and still needy.

"Yes," she admitted.

I heard Cord come into the room behind us.

I shucked my clothes. I couldn't wait another second getting inside her.

"Turn around, beautiful, and grab the headboard."

She did as I said, but eyed me. "You're going to fuck my ass?"

There was concern in her voice, but since she'd moved to comply, she wasn't all that afraid.

I didn't answer as I got my clothes off, and I took a second to take in the way she looked me over, taking in my bare body. I wasn't the least bit modest. If my mate wanted to eye fuck me, I wasn't going to deny her.

"Not today. Soon." *When we claim you*, I wanted to add, but didn't. "For now, I'm going to fuck that newly opened pussy, and I'm going to work my thumb in that ass. Get you used to having both holes filled."

"Both holes?" Cord said as he opened his jeans. "How about all three. Turn this way, baby, and you can have my dick in your mouth too."

He stroked himself from root to tip, and Rachel couldn't miss how hard he was for her. How hard either of us were.

She eyed us, considering, but only for a moment. She turned and faced the side of the bed on all fours. Her perfect tits dangled down, like ripe fruit to be plucked and sucked.

But I needed to be in her now. I'd play with those nipples for hours soon enough.

Cord and I moved into position. I settled on the bed behind her, kneeling. Cord stood in front of her, then set one knee on the bed so he got his dick right in her face.

15

 ACHEL

I LICKED my lips as Cord held the base of his cock to steady it for me. He groaned at the sight, revving my engine even more. As if these two guys didn't already have me feeling hotter, more sexual, more beautiful than I dreamed possible. I was on all fours with two men. One was going to fuck me while fingering my ass, the other was working his dick into my throat.

I had to lower my head to reach Cord's cock, so I went down to my forearms. Nash groaned because I was sure I made quite an invitation from his perspective behind me. I still didn't know how or why these two men had decided I was the one for them, nor did I believe how willing they were to share me, but I wasn't complaining.

They clearly were keepers. Nash had married me without blinking an eye!

Holy shit. I was married to one of these men. That was insane. But Nash was okay with me having sex with not just him, but Cord, too. What man was confident enough to share? These two, and apparently many here in West Springs.

I heard the snap of foil as Nash opened a condom package, and felt a dribble of cool liquid between my butt cheeks. Oh God, lube.

I parted my lips and took Cord deep into my mouth without preamble, making him shout, "Fates!"

I had to open my mouth wide to take him all.

Fates. It was a strange word. I thought I'd heard one of them use it before. I'd have to ask why they said that. Why not *fuck* like most guys? Right now, I couldn't think because Nash was rubbing the head of his sheathed cock over my dripping slit at the same time as Cord cradled the back of my head to guide me over his cock.

Nash gave me another spank before he gripped my hip and eased inside me. I moaned around Cord's cock. It felt so good. Again, the sense of rightness washed through me. It didn't make logical sense, but I had to go with it.

I wanted this. These guys wanted this. What was wrong with it if we were all into it? For once, I was going to trust my gut instead of what everyone else had told me was right. Because I knew my parents and anyone at home or in the sorority would say this was wrong. Or a kinky fling.

Nash pushed his thumb against my slickened anus at the same time as he fed his length into me. As if that wasn't enough to track, Cord gathered my hair in a ponytail at the back of my head, then used it to leverage my face forward and back. It wasn't rough— just gentle controlling—and I loved it.

Nash couldn't seem to hold back, though.

The moment he was fully seated, he let out a growl —almost like a wild animal—and gripped my hip to jackhammer into me. His hips slapped against my ass and he bottomed out inside me. He was so big, I was crammed full. All the while, his thumb filled my ass, stretching my anus that he'd lubed up and providing even more sensory input. More hedonistic pleasure.

"Rachel, you feel so good," he gasped, almost like he couldn't believe it. His words made my pussy gush with even more arousal. Hearing someone finding me so desirable was like a drug, making me euphoric.

"So good," Cord echoed, pulling my mouth over his cock faster now.

Nash pumped his thumb in time with his cock, so I was being fucked by both at the same time.

"I can't get enough," Nash gritted, his fingers tightening around my hip. He slammed in harder and harder, propelling me over Cord's cock, the head working into my throat. My eyes watered, and I breathed through my nose.

"Easy, Nash," Cord warned.

"Fuck, sorry," Nash panted, slowing down and removing his thumb. He paused his movements and instead of pumping his thick cock into me, he simply pulled my hips back to him, which had the added benefit of pulling my mouth back and forth over Cord's length.

"Oh fuck, yes!" Cord groaned.

Nash seemed to be using effort to regulate his breath, as his inhales and exhales fell at a harsh but even pace.

I moaned my own agreement, though it was muffled by Cord's cock.

"I..." Nash struggled to say something.

"Nice and easy," Cord advised. "Gentle with our mate."

Our mate. Another strange choice of words. I liked

the ring of it, though. It sounded... primitive. Animalistic.

I figured that's what we were doing—mating. Like wild things.

"Fuck," Nash muttered. His fingers dug into my hips. I didn't mind—I absolutely loved the intensity— but they would definitely leave marks. "I can't hold back... *Cord.*" He sounded urgent.

"Yes, you can." Cord was firm.

I didn't know why he would need to hold back. Wasn't the point for us all to come? Wouldn't it be incredible if we came together?

I arched my back even more, offering myself for Nash's plunder, and gripped Cord's thighs for stability.

Nash resumed pumping hard, but this time he held my hips close to his to keep from jostling me too much. "Good... so good," he grunted. "So fucking good."

"Yeah, me too." Cord sounded just as lost and almost as out of breath. "I'm going to come," he warned.

Nash reached around the front of my hips and pinched my clit. "You come too, Rachel. Come while Cord spills into your beautiful mouth."

His contact with my clit and the delicious order was all the encouragement I needed. My thighs quaked as my internal walls gripped around Nash's cock and I came harder than I knew was possible.

Cord came at the same time, his salty essence spurting down my throat. He tried to pull out, but I grabbed his ass and pulled him back into my mouth, swallowing down his salty cum.

"Fuck, yeah, Rachel. I love feeling that tight little pussy when it comes," Nash growled. "Give me one more when I finish inside you."

I popped off Cord, licked my lips. "Yes," I said, even though I wasn't sure I could control things, either way. It seemed highly likely, though. My nipples burned, my core was molten. One orgasm was definitely not enough.

"Fates, yes!" Nash cried, drilling into me hard as Cord reached below and pinched both my nipples.

I let out a warbling cry of both need and satisfaction and then Nash shoved in deep, coming hard. I heard a snap of flesh, and a snarl. Cord's hand shot out, reaching above me like he was pushing Nash. Not pushing... I twisted to look, and let out a scream. Cord had Nash by the throat, and Nash's eyes looked wild and silver.

The moment I screamed, both men relaxed. Cord withdrew his hold on Nash and cradled my face. "It's okay," he soothed me.

Nash eased out of me with a soft curse. "I'm sorry, Rachel. Did I hurt you? Was I too rough?"

"No, I'm fine." I was better than fine, although a bit mystified. I was sweaty and achy, my pussy sore from being taken so hard. My jaw was tired from being opened so wide. "What happened?"

"Nothing," both men said at once. Nash moved off the bed and disposed of his condom.

"Nash is just a big guy and has a lot of passion for you," Cord said mildly, as if that somehow explained his need to grip the guy by the throat.

And yet, now they both seemed perfectly in tune. There was no animosity or rivalry that I could sense.

It was weird. I didn't get it.

But then, it wasn't like I had any experience with threesomes. Or sex. Or big, burly cowboys from Wyoming.

So, maybe this was just how these rough cowboys rolled.

"Are you sure you're all right?" Nash scooped me into his arms and crawled up to sit on the bed with his back against the headboard. Cord joined him, and Nash settled me on his lap with my legs spilling over Cord's.

Cord stroked up and down my thigh as Nash propped my back with one strong arm.

"I love you guys," I murmured before I realized what I was saying. *Oh God.* "I mean—"

"Don't take it back," Cord said. Though his voice was soft, the intensity still rang in his words. "Please."

I dragged my lower lip between my teeth as I glanced up at him. I saw everything in his gaze. Heat. Need. Even love, although he hadn't said the words back. I'd *felt* his—their—need for me in what we'd just done. "All right, I won't."

Cord rewarded me with a broad, warm smile.

As my body started to cool, everything inside me warmed. I didn't just feel desired when I was with these men. I felt cherished. Maybe even loved, since I'd just declared it myself. I just wondered if they felt the same way.

"What would it take," Cord said slowly, trailing his fingertips up my calf, "for you to stay in West Springs? I know you're here to find yourself. We understand after seeing that Chester guy—who's a total asshole, by the way—and hearing your call with your father that you have some things to figure out, but can we help make that happen? You don't have to find yourself all alone, do you? What is it about you that needs discovering?"

I smiled at his phrasing. I was sated and content, and his asking me to stay in West Springs didn't sound quite as scary after a few orgasms. It put a lot in perspective. "Well, getting rid of Chester was most of it," I admitted. "Even though that scene at the court-house was unpleasant, I feel a huge weight off my shoulders." I frowned, staring down at my hands. "I don't think I realized how long it had been there. Me leaving the engagement party was running away from it, but today I feel like I finally faced it. So that's already better."

"Okay, what else?" Nash lightly traced my breast with his free hand.

Goosebumps rose on my arms.

I bit my lip and considered. "Well, I'm a pretty shitty waitress, so I don't think I found myself at the diner, as much as I love it—and Bessie."

"You love waitressing?" Cord asked.

I glanced at him through my lashes. "I like the people. The community. I'm earning my own money from hard work, not from my parents. It's... rewarding, but I'll say it again. I'm the worst waitress ever."

Nash's chuckle reverberated through me and he gave me a squeeze. "You're a damn cute one, though."

I laughed and I felt my cheeks heat. I reveled under his praise, even if he was only trying to make me feel better. "Thanks."

"You're looking for a profession?" Cord prompted. "Something *besides* working for Bessie?"

I shrugged and my shoulder slid over Nash's bare chest. "I guess. My parents wanted me to study political science in school, so I could be the wife of a senator—not a senator myself, mind you—but I really have no interest in politics."

"What do you have an interest in?" Nash asked, his finger sliding up and down my arm.

No one had really ever asked me that before. I had always gone along with my parents. Blindly. Meekly. Maybe it was their fault to assume I'd be content with whatever they said when I was little. But it turned into mine when I didn't voice my unhappiness. But, I had never considered myself unhappy until recently. Why had it taken me so long to change from a sheep to a lion?

"I always thought if I had a different life—which, of course, I didn't believe was available to me at the time—I would be a teacher."

"High school?" Nash wondered.

"No, elementary. Kindergarten, maybe. I love kids."

Cord stiffened slightly, and I lifted my gaze to his.

"What?" I asked.

He was silent for a moment. "Rachel... you should know that I can't give you children."

"Can't or won't?"

"Can't, beautiful. I want kids. So much." He raised his hand and tucked a lock of my hair behind my ear. "A little girl with blonde curls."

"How do you know? I mean, did you have measles or something?"

"Or something," he replied. "Instead of speaking clinically, I'll tell you that I'm firing blanks."

I had no idea how he knew that. I was healthy but I couldn't be sure I could get pregnant. Not until I tried.

"The doc likes his facts, beautiful," Nash said and Cord nodded. Cord's shoulders relaxed slightly. It seemed Nash understood better than I did.

Cord set his hand on my thigh and his thumb began to stroke. "I know we're not there yet, and the marriage to Nash was just for show, but if you stayed in West Springs with us, we'd need Nash to have children."

My brows dipped in confusion. It was such a strange way of thinking. "Is that why you were willing to share me with Nash? Because you didn't think you were the full package alone?"

I almost wished I hadn't asked the question—it seemed too intrusive, but Cord immediately nodded.

"Yes. And for other reasons."

What else could there be besides him not being able to have kids?

"What reasons?" I probed.

He and Nash shared a glance. "That's a topic for later. After..."

"After what?"

"After you've accepted that you're ours," Nash supplied. "*Fully* accepted."

"What we just did doesn't count?" I asked.

They shook their heads. "When you're ready, when you accept both of us as yours, then we'll fuck you together," Cord said. "One of us in your pussy, the other in your ass."

My inner walls clenched at the image he painted. I smiled, looking between them to make sure this was just flirting. He was flirting, right? We were naked, and things we'd just done... But they were going to do the double penetration thing?

"She'd better accept us," Cord took on a teasing tone and tweaked one of my nipples, "because I have no intention of ever letting her go."

Yes, they were definitely flirting. And teasing me with something that sounded really darned good. My chest swirled once more with that wonderful warm feeling.

"So, a teacher? That shouldn't be too hard." Nash

looked to Cord. Clearly we were done talking about babies and firing blanks and butt stuff.

"Right," Cord said. "You could probably get your teaching certificate through Granger State. We certainly have an elementary school here."

"Just one?" I laughed.

"Just one." Cord's gaze traced my face. "Could you live in such a small town?"

"Definitely," I answered without hesitation. Strangely, West Springs had felt like home the moment I arrived. Just like Cord and Nash had felt like home the moment I met them.

Everyone was so kind. I absolutely adored the sense of community and taking care of each other they seemed to have here. Plus, if I was going to keep two men—oh God, was I really considering this long term? —it could only happen in a town where threesomes were already common. Caitlyn and Shelby had set my mind at ease that it wasn't all too crazy around here. Bessie, too.

"Good. It's settled, then," Cord said to Nash in that teasing tone. The corner of his mouth tipped up and his gaze raked over me. "We're keeping her."

"Good thing, because I already married her." Nash grinned.

"I still can't believe that. This is all so crazy." I crawled off their laps, ready for a shower.

I wanted—so much—to believe things could just be this easy. That I could follow this good feeling straight into my future. Live with two men. Stay in West Springs. Teach kindergarten.

Could it be that easy? Did people fall in love from a glance across a room? Was there really such a thing as love at first sight? Times two?

It seemed too good to be true. I had a niggling sense there was something off. Something strange. They'd shared infertility and their bodies and their feelings, but there were things they hadn't told me. Something I didn't understand. Cord had pretty much admitted there was more to the picture than he'd explained.

Because it didn't make sense that two strangers would come together with sudden and total willingness to share me. Me!

For life. Yes, it was my fault we'd gotten married, but it had been a lie. Like pretending to date someone. A fake fiancé, like in those romance stories. The marriage could be annulled, but no one could doubt we'd faked what we'd just done.

My phone buzzed from the kitchen, and I scurried in there to pick it up. I wasn't embarrassed being naked in front of Cord and Nash, but I wasn't interested in being seen through his big kitchen windows, so I dashed back into the bedroom. Cord was sitting on the edge of the bed. Nash hadn't moved. I glanced down at the screen. Fourteen messages from Chester.

Ugh. My dad must have given him the number. *Great.*

A thread of anxiety twisted in my gut. What if Nash and Cord knew about my inheritance, too? What if the reason they'd agreed so quickly to share me was because they'd made an arrangement to split it?

No.

I was the one who'd claimed I was married to Nash. That hadn't been his idea, and neither of them had expected Chester to appear. I didn't get the sense either cared about the money. Neither one had even asked about it. Cord had said they had enough to take care of me, but I didn't want to become that trophy wife. I could have been that back in California.

Still, I needed to be careful. I believed there was another piece to this puzzle and until I knew what it was, I probably needed to guard my heart. Because dealing with Chester was one thing. I didn't love him. But these two rugged, sexy cowboys? It seemed I did.

16

ASH

"What's the matter, beautiful?" I asked.

She was staring at her phone, and whatever she saw wasn't making her happy. That was fucking wrong.

No way was anything from the outside world ruining this time. After what we just did, she should be tucked in our arms or passed out. Since she was neither—

"Chester," she muttered.

Fuck. Killing him was becoming a more likely scenario because the dumbass didn't seem to want to take no for an answer. While I understood his obsession with Rachel—I was gone for her, too—she didn't want him. She'd made it clear, more than once.

A guy who didn't take no for an answer was an asshole. A dangerous one. While Chester was a weak little weasel, he was bigger and stronger than Rachel. Had anger fueling him too. Good thing she had two shifter males to protect her now.

Cord grabbed his jeans from the floor and tugged them on. "He called?"

"And texted," she replied, taking a deep breath. I didn't miss the way her tits rose and fell. "A lot."

Fuck.

I climbed from the bed and grabbed her phone. When she looked up at me with wide eyes, I realized my mistake and held it up. "Sorry. Can I see what he sent?"

She nodded and I scrolled through the texts, then moved to her voicemail and hit *Play* on the first one.

"You're being rebellious. I understand. I had a little wild streak after college too. You'll come to your senses soon enough."

Cord raised a brow, and I knew we were thinking the same thing about Chester's message. Would Rachel come to her senses and change her mind about us?

Gibson had told us—ordered us—to mark her and claim her. We were working to win her over to the idea of an 'us.' Did that make us like her ex?

I stabbed the *Play* button for the second voicemail.

"We're not done, Rachel. I don't give a shit if you're married to that fucking country yahoo. You're mine, and that's never going to change."

Cord popped to his feet. I growled and gripped the cell so hard, I felt it crack. He snatched it from my hand.

"I think that's enough of those," he said, being the sane one.

I glanced at Rachel, who'd gone pale. No matter my feelings about the fucker, she came first. She didn't need me to be an overbearing asshole. She already had one of those in her life.

"Turn it off," Rachel said, shaking her head. Her tousled blonde hair slid over her bare shoulders. "He has to realize I'm not his anymore, but I don't have to listen to the fallout."

Damn straight.

Cord must have pushed the right button because the cell went dark and he dropped it onto the bedside table.

"Come on, let's get some food," I said, turning toward the door.

"Naked?" she asked.

I glanced over my shoulder. She was staring at my ass. I raked my gaze over every inch of her perfection, and grinned. "Works for me."

"The doctor says no cooking naked," Cord piped up—referencing himself—and grabbed my t-shirt off the floor and helped Rachel pull it over her head.

My dick lengthened at the sight of her. "Looks better on you, beautiful."

Cord tossed my jeans at me. I caught them right before they hit my face.

Her laughter as she followed Cord out of the bedroom relaxed me and my wolf. That soft sound soothed me. I tugged on my pants, then caught up.

"...live here in West Springs. I think they're going to like you," Cord said, his head stuck in his fridge. He grabbed a package of bacon and a carton of eggs and set both on the counter. Even though it wasn't morning, it seemed we were having breakfast.

"I asked Cord after his family. You know about mine," Rachel said, catching me up. She sat on a stool and leaned on the counter. My t-shirt rode up her thighs and offered me a creamy expanse of her silky skin.

Shit. Family?

"I can't believe you have two dads," she continued.

Cord turned and looked at her as he grabbed a bowl from the cabinet. "That's right."

"It really is a thing around here," she added.

I went to Rachel, I couldn't resist, and stroked her hair. "It's a thing. *Wife.*"

A thrill shot through me saying that. This perfect, gorgeous woman was all mine. Well, halfway.

She tipped her chin up and looked at me. Smiled. "What about you?"

I was mesmerized by her pale eyes. "What about me?"

Parents. Fuck. I didn't realize I was smiling until it slipped. My stomach plummeted, and the scent of bacon filling the air made me feel nauseated.

It was a simple question. Innocent.

I swallowed. "I grew up with my grandparents," I told her, thinking of the tall, proud man and sturdy, but kind woman who'd raised me.

She tipped her head. "Oh?"

I nodded once. "My parents died when I was a baby."

She instantly wrapped her arms around me, pressing her cheek into my bare chest. The feel of her, the comfort, eased the rough emotions. A little. Over her head, I glanced Cord's way. He gave me a look, waiting for me to tell her the rest.

I owed her the truth, even if it was new to me.

"Shelby and her mom are from the same town in Montana as me." Same town, same pack. "They've lived here for a bit now that Shelby's with Gibson and Ben. But Marne had a piece of furniture she needed delivered, and I volunteered. When we met at the barbecue, I'd only been in town a few hours."

"Okay," she said, letting me know she was following but ready for more.

Cord set a glass of orange juice in front of her.

"Interestingly enough, I... I found out I'm from West Springs, too." That was a very mild way of explaining the cluster fuck of my past. "Even though I grew up in Cooper Valley, my fathers were—"

"You have... had two fathers as well?" she asked, holding up her hand.

I swallowed again, hard, as if it was difficult to get these words out. "Yeah. It's as much a surprise for you as it is for me. Turns out, one's an asshole."

She leaned back, looked up at me. "What did he do?"

I took a deep breath, let it out. Said the words that I wasn't sure I could live with. "He killed my mother and other father."

Her eyes widened in surprise. Yeah, that wasn't something that happened every day.

Cord turned off the stove, moved the pan of frying bacon off the burner, and joined us.

"Nash thought his parents were dead," Cord told her.

She looked from Cord to me.

"That's what my grandparents told me," I added. "That I had a mother and only one father. I never knew about the second one until yesterday."

"Wow. That must be hard for you," she said, her eyes full of concern.

I cleared my throat. "Turns out the asshole, Harlan, is still alive."

"He is?" she asked, her eyes widening even more. "You really didn't know?"

"Like you didn't know about the Two Ma—West Springs way," I almost blurted out about the pack, but saved myself just in time. "Neither did I. Cooper Valley's not around the corner, and my grandparents have been gone for a while now."

"Holy shit," she whispered. "You have to see him. Meet him."

I stepped back, as if her words were dirty. "Harlan? No fucking way."

"He's your father," she repeated.

And I looked just like him.

"He's a murderer. I'm already tainted."

"You're not tainted," Cord countered. "We don't take on the sins of our parents."

I wasn't so sure about that. "I want to leave it in the past."

"Turning off my phone isn't going to make Chester go away," Rachel said. "We still have to deal with him."

I loved that she said 'we' even if she probably didn't even realize it.

"You just found out about the guy. Go see him. I'm not saying forgive him, but get... I don't know, clarity." She waved a hand in the air. "Closure."

Clarity? He'd killed my mother and father. Or, *other* father.

Cord was quiet for a moment. "She's right. You need to see him. Meet him. Once, then you can let it go."

"You're Mr. Black and White," I countered. "You need hard facts to analyze, to help base your opinions."

He shook his head. "There aren't opinions, there's only facts. Facts are the truth."

"See?" I said.

He shrugged, not bothered I'd called him out. He knew what he was, how he thought. "Still. You have questions. He's the only person who can answer them."

I did. I had a shit ton of questions. Cord was right. My other parents were long dead. My grandparents gone. I had no one else in my family to ask. I needed to know the truth about who they were.

Hell, about who *I* was.

I wasn't sure if I could ever let it go. Harlan's DNA was mine. Even if I walked away and never saw him again, he was a part of me. I saw it. Felt it in the aggressive way I touched Rachel. In my anger. In my need to tear Chester limb from limb. It was only growing stronger.

17

ACHEL

"If you're my wife, I think we'd better move in together," Nash said the next morning over coffee. It felt so natural to sit around Cord's kitchen table. The three of us fit together, even though it didn't make sense logically.

I smiled. "Move in where?"

"Cord's *casa es mi casa*," he joked.

"Of course you'll move in here," Cord said. "There's no reason to keep your apartment. You *are* married."

I hesitated. Was I moving too fast here? Sure, there

was a piece of paper saying I was Nash's wife. But we hadn't known each other that long, and—

"I mean, you're both welcome to come to Montana, but it feels to me like we belong here. Am I wrong?" Nash spread his hands. "You certainly can't keep renting that apartment of yours if Chester is still sniffing around, trying to prove this marriage is a fraud."

Chester. Fuck.

"Agreed," Cord said, nodding. "We'll go and get your things today."

"When my parents show up, I'll just tell them I married Nash but moved in with Cord? I mean, they're not Mr. and Mrs. Cowboy by any means, but they *will* come to visit me here."

Nash shot me a lopsided grin. "That should go over well."

"They don't have to know it's my house," Cord said, offering an easy answer.

Nash shot him a searching look. "You don't mind?"

Something made me think they were talking about more of a long-term plan than this fake marriage thing. Like I was staying for good. Like the three of us would stay together for the long haul. Long enough my parents would visit, and that was saying a lot.

The thought wasn't the least unsettling, though. I

sort of loved the fantasy of staying in West Springs and having two devoted men, like Caitlyn and Shelby had. It was crazy, but made me feel so cherished. Safe. Protected.

"You're the one who officially married her," Cord reminded. "I'll be the undercover lover. I don't care how the huma—I mean, outside world, sees it. The three of us will know what we are. Our friends will know. That's all that matters to me."

"Undercover lover? Is there a t-shirt for that?" I asked, grinning.

Cord rolled his eyes as he poured himself a cup of coffee.

I shook my head. "It's pretty unbelievable how easily you two roll with this sharing thing."

"Believe it," Nash said. "We're committed to making it work. I know this marriage was for convenience, but I'm all in. Cord, too."

"All in *you*," Cord added.

It was my turn to roll my eyes.

"Let's go move you out of that apartment right now," Cord said. His phone buzzed and he picked it up. "Hi, Caitlyn. No, I'm not coming into the lab today. Did you hear the news? Nash and Rachel just got married." He sent a sexy smirk my way. "No, legally married—except without the wedding. It was a tactical maneuver to throw off a persistent suitor, but we're calling it a win, and moving Rachel into my place today." There was a pause while Caitlyn said something. He said, "Sure. We'll see you later," and hung up.

"Do you work with Caitlyn?" I asked. I'd only met her that short time, and didn't know a thing about her.

"Yes. She's a biologist and we're working on a wolf DNA project together." Cord sent a glance Nash's way that I couldn't quite interpret. Like Nash should know what that meant or something.

I looked at Nash for more information, but his face remained blank. "I only know her from the kiss-off in front of Shelby's house," he said.

I looked back to Cord. "So you're a family practice doctor and a researcher?"

He shrugged. "Well, the research is my pet project. The family practice is my main source of income, but having Caitlyn's focus on the research has really helped me move it forward."

Impressive. "Wow. There's so much I don't know about you."

Cord and Nash shared another glance and Cord got up from the table. "We've got all the time in the world to share. Come on, let's head over to your place."

"I can follow in my truck. Plenty of room in the flatbed," Nash said.

"You're forgetting how I got to West Springs," I reminded. "Everything I own will fit in one suitcase and a grocery bag."

Nash laughed. "In that case, we can all ride together." He slid my chair back like a gentleman and kissed me when I stood.

It was sweet. The kind of thing my father did for my mother. It felt natural when Nash did it, but if Chester had ever done such a thing, I would have rebuffed the attention. It seemed so obvious now that I just was never attracted or interested in Chester. I had tried to make myself believe I was, but there was absolutely nothing there.

As for Nash and Cord, there was definitely *something*.

———

IT TOOK us all of forty-five minutes to pack my apartment, and then the guys helped me clean the place so I could get my full deposit back.

When a knock came at the door, I frowned, fearing it might be Chester again.

"Hang on, I'll get it," Nash said protectively, as if he had the same concern.

"Congratulations!" a friendly voice rang out. Caitlyn and Wade stood in the doorway carrying a bottle of champagne and a fruit basket. "This was all I could get on short notice," Caitlyn said apologetically.

I laughed, and accepted the gifts and a hug. "Come on in. You know it's not a real marriage, right?"

Beside me, Nash bristled, but didn't say anything.

"It's a good excuse to celebrate," Caitlyn replied. "You've got one legal husband and an illegal one—I'd say you're doing pretty good!"

I looked over at Nash and Cord, and my insides melted. "Yeah, I guess I am."

Caitlyn went to the kitchen cupboard and pulled out five mismatched glasses. "Let's have a toast."

"Right now? It's the middle of the afternoon," I protested with a laugh.

Wade worked the cork out from the top of the bottle until it made a *pop*. "No better time than the present." He filled the five glasses, and we each took one.

"To impromptu weddings," Caitlyn said.

"To West Springs' newest threesome." Wade lifted his glass.

"To Rachel," Cord said.

"To Rachel," Nash repeated.

For some ridiculous reason, my eyes got wet. Even though this wasn't a real marriage, even though there hadn't been a wedding, the feelings were just as strong as if I were standing there in a wedding dress under a country club flower arch.

The complete opposite of how I'd felt at my surprise engagement party.

"To my two fabulous boyfriends, or I should say, husbands, and to new friends." I clinked my glass against all of theirs and took a sip of the bubbly.

I looked around at them, memorizing the moment. Whether things here in West Springs lasted or not, this was a memory I never wanted to forget. I felt alive for the first time in my life. Like my life, my future, had just begun.

I had friends and lovers. I felt... included.

Nash and Cord each put an arm around me and I tipped my head up to one, then the other for a champagne-flavored kiss. "I love you guys," I murmured.

"I love you, Rachel," Cord answered.

"I love you." Nash stroked my cheek with the backs of his fingers, and smiled.

Was this real?

18

ASH

RACHEL WAS in our bed officially now that she was out of her apartment. Cord's bed, technically, but the longer we had our mate between us, the more his house became ours. All three of us. Even while we talked and fucked and slept and ate and fucked some more, I thought about what she and Cord had said about meeting Harlan.

I'd never had questions about my parents before. Sure, I'd wondered what they'd been like, since I'd been a baby when they'd died. I'd never imagined having a second father and him be alive.

The picture Wade had shared was irrefutable. I was Harlan's. We didn't need any of Cord's scientific data to know.

I couldn't move forward without learning about the past. I didn't think I was going to like what I found out, but the *what ifs* were going to fuck with me.

I gave in after two days. A two-day honeymoon of sorts. Word had spread through West Springs about the impromptu wedding. No doubt Bessie and Norma together were able to get the news of the event to every shifter in the pack. Bessie had called Cord and told him that Rachel shouldn't be at work for a week. I wasn't sure who'd called about the doctor's office, but someone was filling in with patients for Cord.

I'd texted Rand and given him a heads up, but a vague one. Only that I'd found my mate and was staying for a while in West Springs. I was sure he was curious to know more, but had given me space. I had no doubt he remembered what it had been like when first meeting Natalie.

I called Wade and got Harlan's address. I took my truck and headed out, following the provided directions. Two hours after kissing Rachel goodbye, I pulled up in front of a small cabin in the middle of nowhere.

Cooper Valley was a small town. So was West

Springs. Here? There was no town nearby. Nothing was out here except windswept prairie and a patch of trees indicating a creek or other water source. There were no mountains, even. This part of Wyoming was vastly different. Rugged, but in a barren way.

Since the cabin sat on open land with no neighbors for miles, I was sure Harlan had heard my approach. Even if he hadn't, his dog had. An enormous German Shepherd came tearing around from the back of the house, barking and snarling like she was ready to kill.

I turned off the engine and climbed out. "Sit," I commanded the dog sharply, infusing my voice with alpha command.

Recognizing my dominance, she whimpered and dropped to her haunches, lowering her head. She had grey around her muzzle and threaded through her black ears.

It wasn't common for wolf shifters to keep dogs, but some did. Living out here, banished from his pack and so far away from humans, Harlan's dog kept him sane, I imagined.

"Good girl," I murmured and looked around.

The place was small, but tidy. The grass around the house was trimmed, the roof and log walls in good shape. An old truck was parked in front of a barn, although I didn't see any livestock. No fencing for horses. Not even a coop for chickens.

Anyone who lived out here wanted to be alone. I'd passed the nearest grocery store fifteen miles back, and that hadn't been a big box business, only a small mom and pop shop.

The place was unnerving. Fucking lonely as hell. Once winter set in... fuck. I thought of Rachel and her warmth, her heat. Fire. The way she slept with her head on my chest. Even Cord made things better. He was becoming a friend. A good one. My partner in keeping our mate happy and satisfied. Now, I couldn't imagine being with Rachel solo.

"Lost?" A deep voice had me turning on the dirt drive.

A man wearing jeans and a heavy plaid shirt came from the back of the house, taking the same path the dog had, but slower. He was tall, but his shoulders were slightly curved. His hair leaned toward gray, but I couldn't miss the sandy blond. The same color as mine. The dog got up and ran to him, licking his fingers where they hung by his side.

He stroked her head without taking his gaze from me. When his eyes met mine, he stopped, about fifteen feet away. His dog sat beside him, eyes also trained on me, a low growl in her throat now that she was with her master.

Harlan's nostrils flared like he was taking in my scent. No doubt he recognized I was a shifter.

I removed my hat, let the sun hit my face full on.

His eyes widened and he stared at me as if he'd seen a ghost.

Or a younger version of himself.

"I'm thinking you know who I am," I said.

He didn't look away, didn't even blink, as he shook his head.

There was no surprise reunion. Hugs. Tears.

"No." His hand came up and he ran it over his mouth.

"I'm Cathryn Taggart's son."

He said something, but it got caught on the wind. That same breeze ruffled my hair.

"Didn't... didn't know she had one."

"I thought my father was dead," I said.

He continued to stare, then finally blinked.

"No. I'm alive." The words lacked energy.

"I meant Noble Mead. He's dead. Cathryn, too."

"I know."

I wanted to reach right out and snap Harlan's neck. But no. I was here for closure, but not that kind. I'd come this far to hear what he had to say about their death. Judge for myself.

"What'd they do, try to tell someone about how you were abusive? That why you killed them?"

His ruddy skin paled slightly, but he didn't seem surprised by my harsh words.

"Come inside. That's a cold wind."

I didn't feel it. I didn't feel much of anything but my hatred for him. The one who made me. Whose blood flowed through my veins.

Fuck me, it was the blood I'd pass down to any pups we had with Rachel. Because the *we* in that thought was me. Cord couldn't have kids. Only I could. How did I tell Rachel I didn't want to pass on any of my messed up DNA?

He turned and strode toward the house, expecting me to follow. His dog stayed and growled at me, but Harlan snapped, "Come, Dolly." She immediately stood and raced to his side.

Fuck.

Well, I'd come this far. I wasn't going to leave now. He knew that.

I entered his house, the wood-burning stove heating the main room. The furniture was old, but well-maintained. It was clear he lived alone. There were no photos on the walls. No mementos. From where I stood, I could see into the dated kitchen, and a hint of a bathroom off to the right. There was a short hallway where I assumed the bedroom was. I doubted there was a basement, and no stairs led to a second floor.

Harlan grabbed a log from the small pile in the corner, opened the door to the stove, and tossed it in. It crackled and the scent of wood filled the room. There was no TV but a book was on the table, as well as a pair of reading glasses. Shelves lining the wall were filled with paperbacks.

Funny, I wouldn't have guessed a violent wolf shifter would be a reader.

"What's your name?" Harlan asked, moving around the sofa and to a recliner. He dropped into it and held out a hand for me to take a seat.

I set my hat on the coffee table and settled on the far side of the couch.

"Nash."

"You look just like me." He couldn't stop staring.

I could only nod.

"What made you come now, after all this time?" he asked.

"All this time? I didn't fucking know you existed until a few days ago. Hell, I didn't even know I was from Two Marks," I replied, meaning the pack.

"Where have you been?"

"Montana. With my grandparents."

"Cathryn's parents? All this time? Fates—" His eyes widened and he went white. "Were you in the car?" he choked. "How did you survive the crash?"

My eyes narrowed to slits. I dragged short breaths through my flared nostrils. "So you *were* there," I said. I wanted to yell at him. Beat him up. Kill him for harming my parents. But no. That aggression was *his* aggression. I couldn't feed it. I didn't want to become him.

Harlan still looked pale, like he was going to be sick. "Yeah, I was there." His voice cracked.

I huffed. My blood boiled, and I struggled to sit still. "Were you trying to kill me, too?"

"I didn't mean to kill anyone!" he shouted, his eyes flashing silver.

I felt my wolf answer his, my vision sharpening and doming as my eyes probably changed to the same exact color. I could tear him limb from limb right now at the slightest provocation. Or shift, and tear his throat out with my fangs.

Except Harlan's eyes had already flashed back to blue, and I realized what I saw on his face wasn't rage or violence.

It looked more like anguish.

"I didn't know you existed, son."

"Don't call me *son*," I gritted, my hands curled into fists. "My mother hid my existence from you. When you came to Wolf Ranch, she probably gave me to my grandparents to hide from you. Whatever you did, she clearly didn't want you to be my father, and that sure as hell won't change now."

"I hurt her, it's true." Harlan appeared haunted. "I hurt them both. But I didn't mean to."

"*What did you do?*" In an effort to keep control, I lowered my voice to barely more than a harsh whisper.

Harlan stared at me for a long moment. Then he said, "You stink of a human female."

At the mention of my mate, I wanted to tear his head off. I surged to my feet. "You'll speak with respect about my mate, or I'll break every bone in your body."

Harlan also rose, but he appeared more alarmed than ready to war with me. "Your mate is human?" That haunted look returned to his face. "Fuck. And you haven't marked her yet, have you?"

My sight sharpened to wolf vision again. "Shut your fucking mouth about my mate!" My wolf was barely in check, the need to protect my mate was so strong. Thank Fate I refused to let Rachel come along today, or Harlan would already be dead.

"Nash, son, you need to be careful when you claim

her. If she's human, then she'll be fragile. You need to—"

I closed the distance between Harlan and me, fisting his shirt and getting right into his face. The dog growled, but I didn't pay it any attention. "I told you not to call me *son*. And don't talk about my mate."

"This aggression? This is what happened to me with your mother. I need to tell you—"

"I don't want to hear it!" I exploded. I wasn't being rational anymore. For some reason, my wolf was frantic to protect my mate, even though she wasn't here. Having Harlan—a dangerous shifter who had just about confessed to murdering my parents—even mention her name was driving my wolf insane.

The dog snarled and snapped, but Harlan bit out a sharp command and she stopped her lunge for me.

Realizing I was becoming exactly what I feared, I turned on my heel and stalked out the door.

"Hang on, Nash," Harlan called to my back. He followed me, but I didn't care. "I need to tell you what happened. It relates to your mate."

"Stop talking about my mate!" I started jogging now, just needing to get in the truck and away from my sperm donor.

"It's fucking important, Nash! I don't want you to hurt her!"

"That won't happen," I snarled as I climbed in the truck and slammed the door.

Harlan slapped his palm against my closed window as the truck roared to life. "Listen to me, Nash. I need to tell you—"

"Go to hell, old man!" I yelled, peeling out in the dirt as I took off.

As I drove down the long dirt road, I got out my phone and dialed Cord. When he answered, I bit out, "It's over. I can't do it."

"Can't do what?"

"I can't be with you and Rachel. I'm way too much like Harlan." I gripped the steering wheel so hard, I feared it would snap. I still didn't have my wolf under control. "He warned me that I'd hurt her, and I know it's true. And Cord—Rachel's human. My mother was a shifter, and Harlan... Fuck. If I did anything to damage our female, she wouldn't heal from it."

"Hang on," he said, his voice calm. "Where are you? What are you doing right now?"

"I'm driving back to Wolf Ranch. I need to get the hell away from you and Rachel before something terrible happens."

"Come back to my place. We'll talk it over."

I sucked my breath in and out through clenched teeth. "I can't risk it."

"Go to my place," he repeated. "You need to at least tell Rachel goodbye. Hurting her emotionally would be just as unforgivable."

Fuck.

The thought of hurting my mate made my chest throb.

"Okay," I agreed, wiping my mouth with the back of my hand. "I'll say goodbye. Then I'm leaving for Wolf Ranch. Tonight."

 ORD

GODDAMMIT.

I hung up the phone and shoved it in my pocket. I'd walked out on my deck so Rachel wouldn't overhear the conversation, and I stepped back inside now.

Fuck!

This entire time, I'd been as worried about Nash as he'd been about himself, but now that he was actually walking away, it felt all wrong.

Not just because I couldn't give Rachel pups. He was an integral part of our threesome. It was in our DNA to want to mate in threes, and he was my scent match. A brother of sorts, even if we hardly knew each other. My wolf trusted him, even if I wasn't completely sure.

But I found it hard to believe he was really a danger. Yes, he had a hard time holding back with Rachel. Sexually, he was rougher and more dominant than I was. It would be an issue if Rachel wasn't aroused by it, but she was. She liked to feel his power and control. His intensity. It was how he shared how he felt for her. As if he couldn't help himself. That was Nash, the man. His wolf was also involved, desperate to claim and mark her. Yet his urge to protect was just as strong as mine. Strong enough to drive away to save her.

Hell, the guy had asked me to put him down if it ever looked like he'd hurt our mate. So his intentions were pure.

"Everything okay?" Rachel asked. She was sitting at my kitchen table with my laptop, researching the requirements to get a teacher's certificate. After our talk, it was something she felt good about. Excited.

Things had seemed perfect—they were moving in the direction of Nash and me claiming her for good, and now this.

I had no idea what had happened when he'd met Harlan, but it hadn't been good.

"Not exactly." I wanted to be as honest as I could. It already bothered the fuck out of me that we couldn't tell Rachel what we were yet. "Things didn't go well for Nash with his father. He's on his way back here, and is upset."

Her eyes widened and she closed the lid on the laptop to give me her full attention. "What happened?"

I shrugged. "He didn't say. You and I have parents. Yours love you maybe a little too much."

She nodded and laughed in agreement.

"Mine aren't quite so... overbearing, but Nash never knew his. Now, well, one visit doesn't make a father and son a family."

"You're right."

I ran a hand over my face. Considered. "I need to run out to Gibson's place for a bit, but I'll be back when Nash gets here, okay?"

I didn't know what Nash just found out about his father, but I couldn't rely on his emotional response. If it was bad enough to run back to Montana, then I needed to be armed with knowledge to convince him to stay. I needed facts. Wade hadn't shared many facts, mostly what his parents remembered.

"Sure." She stood and wrapped her arms around

me. I'd never get tired of that—her comfort, and her seeking it in return.

"He's going to need you." I kissed the top of her head. I didn't want to tell her Nash planned on breaking things off. I needed to get clear on the situation first, then I could figure out how to handle it.

Rachel's brow furrowed in concern as she looked up at me. "Okay. Of course I'll be here for him. Whatever he needs."

I leaned down and took her lips with mine, inhaling her sweet scent. "I'll be back soon."

Once in my truck, I called Gibson.

"Have you claimed your mate?" he answered.

I ground my teeth. "Not yet. And the wheels are falling off the wagon, to be honest. I was wondering if I could come to your place to read the old pack meeting records or private pack logs that your father kept."

There was silence for a moment. "What are you looking for?"

"Information on Nash's dad. Harlan. I've heard the stories, but I want the facts."

"What, specifically, is your concern?"

I stepped on the gas in frustration, as if getting to Gibson's sooner would solve this shitstorm. "Wade updated you?"

"He did."

"Nash went to meet Harlan. Now he's convinced he's an unsuitable mate, like his father. I want to see if I can find out what really happened. I can trust your father's take on it more than the elders' gossip, if you know what I mean."

Even though the information I was requesting was his father's, the previous alpha, it was Gibson's call on whether the information could be shared. While it wasn't confidential, it was considered private. Privileged, even. "Absolutely," he said.

Inwardly, I sighed. Outwardly, I released my death grip on the steering wheel, but I didn't slow down.

"I'll pull the logs. You got a date? A year?"

"Nash is around thirty, so let's start with the year before he was born."

"I'll get them out. See you in a few."

I drove the rest of the way to Gibson's house and knocked on the door, waiting for his voice to shout 'come in' before I entered. I found him in his office, an old notebook open on his desk. He was poring over it.

He glanced up at me as I came in, then back at the book. "Sounds like Harlan was nearly moon mad when he marked Nash's mother. It wasn't a domestic abuse situation—it was a rough claiming," Gibson said. "Noble was in the middle of it, so of course, he took some injuries as well. Harlan shifted and ran into the woods and disappeared for days. Everyone was calling for him to be put down for moon madness. Noble definitely wanted him put down—he was angry as hell, and protective of his new mate. The whole pack was up in arms over it and Harlan really looked like the bad guy. My father wasn't so quick to condemn him though."

He pointed to a spot in the book. I stood on the opposite side of his desk but couldn't read it upside down.

"My fathers hunted Harlan, fully prepared to put him down if he'd gone feral, but he hadn't. They found him holed up in a cave in human form."

"Shit." I rubbed a hand across my face imagining the scene. "That's almost worse."

"Exactly. Moon madness can be explained—it's an illness—but a wolf hurting his two mates and *not having it*? That doesn't happen. At least, not in this pack. I guess he begged my dad to put him down. He was deeply ashamed about what happened. My father refused." Gibson handed me the notebook, and I skimmed the story for myself.

"So that's why Cathryn and Noble left for Montana?" I asked, glancing at Gibson when I'd finished.

"Looks like it," he replied, sitting back in his chair.

"No one but my father could accept the fact that Harlan hadn't meant to hurt Noble and Cathryn, and that he was safe once his mate had been marked."

Gibson pulled out a second notebook.

"This one is from the following year. It has the report of the accident in Cooper Valley. It sounds as if Harlan learned they were in Montana. He'd gone to try to fix things, but according to him, Noble and Cathryn took off in a car. He followed. My father writes that Harlan swore he didn't run them off the road. There was a boulder that had rolled down with the rain into the road, a mudslide, and Noble swerved to miss it. The roads were icy. Their car shot off the road and crashed into the ravine below. That's Harlan's story, anyway. Again, my father seemed inclined to believe him. There's no actual log of him ever being banished." Gibson handed me the second notebook. "I suspect he banished himself out of grief and shame."

"What about Nash? He had to be the reason they fled," I said.

Gibson nodded, his look grim. "They must have been afraid Harlan would harm the baby. Cathryn had Nash in Montana in secret. There's no record here." He tapped the journal. "They must have found out Harlan was searching and fled, leaving Nash with Cathryn's parents."

"They died, and what? Harlan never even knew he had a kid?"

"Looks that way. My father believed in Harlan. If he'd known about a baby, he wouldn't have kept a shifter from his infant son."

What a twisted tale. "That means Nash's grandparents thought Harlan to be guilty and a danger, because Nash never knew of him."

Gibson sighed. "Don't be angry with them. They did what they thought was right. To protect a cub is crucial."

Harlan never knew about his own son. Nash never knew he had a second father who was still alive. So much secrecy. So much time lost.

"I can't have pups," I admitted. A flush spread across my face as I admitted that shame. I wasn't even sure why I did it.

Gibson eyed me, leaned forward. "You're sure?"

I nodded. I was the only sure person in this pack. I relied on facts, not guesses.

"So?" he said.

I frowned.

"You're the pack scientist. You are well aware of the reason Two Marks shifters mate with two males."

"Because of the lack of females," I replied.

He shrugged. "That's one answer. Perhaps another

is in case there's a match like yours. You can't put the puck in the goal, but your scent match can."

My mouth fell open at his analogy. "You been watching hockey?" I asked.

A slow grin spread across my alpha's face. "You're the doctor. I could say something about sperm and implantation, but that doesn't sound as fun."

I laughed. "Fine. I'm firing blanks, and Rachel loves kids. Wants them. I can't give them to her."

"Again, so? I'm not sure why you're telling me this now. The three of you are nothing like Nash's parents. Their story is tragic, but singular. Regardless, Nash's soldiers can... whatever. He can be the one to make the pups. There's no shame in your situation." He studied me. "You feel shame, though."

I looked down. Shrugged. "I did, because I didn't have a scent match and couldn't give a female pups."

"Now you have a scent match and a mate. What the hell's the problem?"

"I thought it was the fact that I had an unstable scent match, but I just proved that false."

My research into the past offered the truth. Nash wasn't a danger. He was an asset. Gibson was right. I couldn't knock up my mate. Nash could. And we'd have fun doing it.

"May I take these?" I held up both the notebooks,

suddenly relieved and eager to get back to my mate. "I'd like to show Nash. I *need* to show him."

Gibson nodded. "Of course, just make sure I get them back as soon as you're finished. I really should have Wade digitize all those so they're never lost or misplaced."

"I will bring them back tomorrow."

Fuck. I hoped it wasn't too late.

If our old alpha had believed Harlan, I was inclined to, as well. Which meant Nash didn't have violence bred into him. Only a threat of moon madness.

In fact, the biggest danger was him walking away from his mate right now.

He'd probably go mad within the month if I let that happen.

I jumped in my truck, setting the books on the seat beside me. I needed to be back at my place before he talked to Rachel. Nash needed to know the truth.

 ACHEL

WHEN I HEARD the sound of tires on the gravel, I grabbed a sweater and went outside. Cord had me worried about Nash, and I wanted to be there to greet him.

Nash climbed out, looking a bit wild—like he was responding to some unseen emergency. His gait was jerky, his shoulders hitched up. It was the grim expression on his face that really worried me, though.

"Nash." I jogged forward and slid my arms around his waist to hug him.

He hesitated before he put his arms around me,

which wasn't like him. Not at all. I didn't like him tentative. I liked his firm hold, his sure kisses. His intense need for me.

"Hey, what happened? Cord said things didn't go well with your dad?"

"He's not my dad. My dad died when I was a baby," he said through gritted teeth. "Rachel... I can't do this with you."

I went still. Looked up. "What?"

"Harlan is fucking dangerous, which means I am, too. I can't be your mate."

There was that word again. "My what?"

He took off his hat and ran a hand through his blond hair. "Your husband. I can't do it. It's not safe for you."

"Of course it is. You wouldn't hurt me. I don't understand. I know you're a little rough, but I like it."

"Rough?"

Another vehicle approached, and I was relieved when Cord parked. He'd be able to talk some sense into Nash. He was there when we had sex. He knew I liked Nash's more intense play.

Except, it wasn't Cord's truck. I didn't recognize the white compact car that pulled in.

Oh God.

I did recognize the driver. It was Chester behind

the wheel, and he was glaring at the way I was in Nash's arms.

Chester showing up was *not* what we needed right now.

When Nash turned to see who arrived, his body went rigid and a menacing snarl came out of his throat. He stepped in front of me to block Chester's view. "We made it pretty fucking clear. You're not welcome here, buddy," Nash told him when he got out of the car.

I peeked around Nash's large body. Chester appeared even wilder, and in a worse mental state than Nash. I'd never seen him so riled. His face was flushed, his hair disheveled, and his clothes were rumpled and stained, like he'd been wearing them for days. I'd never seen him less than perfect.

"Chester, Jesus," I said. "You look terrible. When's the last time you slept?"

"Get back in the fucking car and drive away," Nash barked. He was way more aggressive than the last time we saw Chester, but it made sense. Chester had been harassing me by phone for days now. He'd called me more times in forty-eight hours than he had the entire four years I was at Stanford.

He'd been warned to leave me alone. I'd made it clear I wanted nothing to do with him.

"No," Chester said, tucking his hand in his jacket pocket. "I'm not leaving without Rachel."

"Oh yes, you are." I heard Nash's knuckles crack as his fingers squeezed into fists.

"Oh, I am not," he snapped. "She's *mine*. She was meant to marry me. Her inheritance was supposed to start my political career—her grandfather told me as much before he died."

"Chester, I'm not marrying you!" I shouted. Nash had his arm across my chest, but I was no longer behind him. "Nash is my husband, and that's final. I love him. I want to be with him. Not you. You'll find donors for your campaign, like most politicians do. You don't need me."

"I do need you!" he shouted, a bit of spittle flying from his mouth. The guy looked insane. Seriously insane. "I have debts. Gambling debts. I can't get out of them. I need that fucking money!"

Jesus.

My stomach churned. The ground seemed to tilt.

Chester had a gambling problem?

God, what a con. He'd never been anything but a shark, preying on me for my money. He didn't want me. He never had.

"Not my problem," I said firmly, crossing my arms over my chest. "You heard Nash. Get back in your rental car, and drive yourself out of my life. For good this time."

Chester took a step closer. "Not. Happening. Rachel, step away from this loser."

I frowned, confused, until I saw him draw his hand from his pocket. Oh God—he had a gun!

The sound of a third car turning down the long dirt drive made Chester turn. Nash rushed forward, faster than I would have believed possible, but Chester turned back and fired right before Nash reached him. He pulled the trigger again and again.

I screamed, as if the sound of my voice might stop those bullets.

They hit Nash square in the chest.

One. Two. Three. Four. Five.

Yet Nash still kept going after Chester, cocking his fist and starting to swing, but his body finally crumpled and dropped to the ground before he could complete the action.

"Nash!" I shrieked, running forward. My lover—my husband—was gasping, choking in rage, still focused on getting to Chester.

I dropped to my knees beside Nash, set my hands to the bleeding on his chest, but Chester pressed the gun to my forehead. I froze.

Sweat slid down my back, and my heart raced.

"No," Nash gasped, collapsing completely in the grass.

"Get up and get in the car." Chester shot a look over his shoulder at the old beat-up truck approaching. "*Now!*"

Tears coated my cheeks. I wanted to tell him no, but some sense of self-preservation kicked in. I stood, and ran to the car. The moment I was in it, Chester dove behind the wheel and took off, backing up at full speed, whizzing past the old truck.

I looked over my shoulder to see Nash, but the truck blocked my view. In my shock, I saw the driver.

He looked familiar, but I was sure I didn't know him.

He had to help Nash, to call an ambulance for him. He had to save my husband.

But the truck turned around in the drive, and followed us.

"Nash," I sobbed, my heart torn to shreds.

Chester skidded around the corner out onto the forest road, but the old beat-up pickup continued to chase after us. I wasn't watching where we were headed, but I turned when Chester spoke.

"We're getting married, Rachel."

He was sweating, his eyes wild. The gun was in his

lap. It jumped when the car hit a rut in the road. Chester swerved, barely keeping control of the car.

"I am *married*," I replied.

"Not anymore you're not," he countered, patting the gun. "You're a widow. We're getting a license, and you're going to be Mrs. Chester Barnes before nightfall."

A widow. *A widow.* I saw Nash get shot. Not once, but several times. Saw the blood. Saw him fall to the ground, gasping. I looked down at my palms, coated red.

Chester took a sharp turn down another dirt road. I had no idea where we were. An ambulance would take forever to get to Nash. Then the ride to the hospital. As far as I knew, Cord was the only doctor in the area, and he was with Gibson. Granger was the closest bigger town. The closest hospital.

Nash was dead. He couldn't be anything else.

Tears slid down my cheeks.

"I'll give you whatever you need to pay off your debts," I said.

He glanced my way, his eyes narrowed with hatred. "I want it all. The inheritance. The trust fund. All of it. We're marrying."

"We don't even like each other."

He laughed and braked hard as we came to a turn.

The back end of the car slid. "I killed one person. You're next. All I need is the paper, not you. Once we're wed, I don't need you any longer."

I snatched the gun from his lap. While I knew he needed me alive to marry me, he was crazy, and I didn't trust him.

"Hey!" He grabbed for me and took his eyes off the road.

We fumbled, the gun falling to the floorboard at my feet.

Chester slammed on the brakes and the tires lost their grip on the loose gravel. He overcompensated and turned the wheel hard, which didn't help. The car slid sideways into a ditch.

I flew forward, then slammed back at the impact. Chester hit his head on the side window and I blinked, taking a second to recover. The old truck that had been following us skidded to a halt, cutting off our path back onto the road.

The car was at an angle and I threw the door open and flung myself out, eager to get away from Chester.

"Get back in here!" he shouted, opening his own door. "Rachel! Get back."

I ran toward the old truck as the driver stepped out of it.

The crack of a gunshot made me stumble. Dammit! Why hadn't I grabbed that gun first?

I screamed, the image of Nash falling to the ground replaying in my mind, but the bullet just punctured the old truck. No one was hit.

"Get in the truck!" The driver launched from the vehicle, running straight toward Chester.

And then I thought I must have lost my mind, because it seemed like the man changed into a giant silver wolf mid-air. The wolf snarled, jaws open wide. Its two giant front paws landed on Chester's shoulders and knocked him backward, then its teeth snapped around his throat.

Rather than watch the result of the attack, I heeded the man's directive and ran for the truck. I climbed in and locked the doors, every part of me shaking.

"This isn't happening," I muttered to myself. Because I'd just seen a man turn into a wolf.

And that's when it hit me—why the man looked familiar. He was an older version of Nash. It must be his father!

Nash. I covered my mouth and choked on a sob. Nash lay bleeding out, back at Cord's house. Dead or dying.

A sharp rap came at my window and I shrieked

again before I realized it was Nash's father. "It's all right. You're safe now." His shirt was in tatters across his chest and there was blood smeared across his jaw.

"Wh-who are you?" I asked through the window, even though I was already sure I knew.

He turned his blue gaze toward me as I rolled down the window. "Harlan Fisher."

"Nash's father," I whispered.

Glancing at my hands, I saw the blood. Nash's blood. "He's dead." The tears came then, along with an adrenaline drop.

"I don't think he's dead. Let's go see about him, honey," he said, his voice calm and almost soothing. "Stay here while I get some clothes from the back of the truck. Everything's going to be okay."

I felt safe with him, and had to wonder if that meant if the story Nash knew about the man was wrong.

I put my hands over my face and cried.

It didn't matter. Nothing mattered. Nash was dead. I hadn't meant to marry him, but now, I was so glad I was his wife. If all I had were a few days with him, then I'd treasure that time. Family wasn't just blood, it was who you let into your life. My parents' love was overbearing, and I had to wonder if it was conditional on being the person they wanted. With Nash and

Cord, they wanted me no matter what. A horrible waitress. A virgin. A lost woman trying to find herself.

I was a horrible waitress. I wasn't a virgin any longer. And I wasn't a lost woman anymore. I'd found myself. In Cord and Nash.

Harlan, now dressed, climbed in the cab of the truck and started it up.

"I... you're..." I took a breath, still trying to process what I'd seen. "You're a wolf."

He shot me a sidelong glance, then dragged a hand through his hair. "Hell. You didn't know." He turned the truck around and started toward Cord's place.

"What happened to Chester?" I almost didn't want to know.

"He won't bother you or anyone else, honey. I took care of it."

"It?"

"Him. He tried to kill my son, and he kidnapped his mate. Tried to kill you."

That's when it hit me. He said *mate*. Not *wife*. "Nash is a wolf."

"He is."

O.M.G.

A... wolf?

Then I sat up straighter. "You said Chester *tried* to kill your son."

"That's right. Tried. I'm sure Nash is feeling like shit right now, but he'll be on the mend by the time we get back to him. Unless he took one to the head." He sent a worried glance my way. "Did he?"

"No." I blinked. My mouth fell open like I was a fish. "But he was shot," I finally said.

"Bullets don't usually kill wolf shifters."

My heart took wing and flew. Nash wasn't dead?

"Your mates are probably going out of their minds right now." He turned down Cord's driveway. Cord's truck was there and he was kneeling by Nash's side, right where I'd left Nash. Cord stood as Harlan approached, then jogged toward the truck. And me.

My gaze went to Nash's figure on the ground. He pushed up to his forearms to see our approach. Harlan was right. Nash wasn't dead.

Thank God!

I tumbled out of the truck into Cord's arms, then ran for Nash.

21

ASH

"Rachel." I tried to get to my feet, but the bullet holes in my torso slowed me down. There were just so damn many of them, and they went through vital organs. I was gonna feel weak for a day or two. I dropped back to one knee and Rachel threw herself on her knees in front of me.

Her scent surrounded me. Her hands carefully ran over my face and shoulders.

I raked my gaze over her, afraid she wasn't real.

"Thank fuck," I murmured, reaching for her face.

"How—" I lifted my gaze and took in Harlan, approaching with Cord. I blinked in confusion. I really had lost a lot of blood. It was affecting my brain function. "What happened? Where's the fucker who took you?"

I couldn't relax until I knew he couldn't harm Rachel again.

"I took care of him," Harlan said, matter-of-factly. I didn't like the guy, but if he'd saved my mate and finished that Chester asshole, then I owed him my thanks.

"You're a wolf," Rachel crooned, holding my face between her two hands and weeping. I focused back on her, which was easy to do, knowing she was safe.

"Shit. Yeah. We both are." I lifted my chin in Cord's direction and tried not to wince. "And you're our mate."

"Your mate," she repeated softly, some form of understanding blooming in her face. "I'm your mate. Oh, Nash, I thought you were dead, but Harlan said you're going to heal?"

"That's right, beautiful. It'll take more than a few bullets to finish me."

Rachel laugh-wept harder. "You being wolves makes so much sense. I kept thinking there was something I didn't understand around here."

"We hoped to tell you soon," Cord explained. "Come on, let's get Nash inside." He and Harlan came and hoisted me up by my arms so I could find my feet. With shifter strength, I was sure one of them could have carried me inside alone, but they knew better than to hurt my dignity in front of Rachel. I would heal faster in wolf form, but Rachel was here, and we had to talk.

They steadied me as I staggered toward the house.

"You were waiting to be sure I'd stick around to tell me you were werewolves?" Rachel asked.

"Shifters," I clarified. The two shifters dropped me in a leather armchair while Rachel ran for a towel to mop up the blood. It had pretty much stopped now, but I was covered in it.

Cord stood, his eyes assessing. The doctor in him was in control now, but there wasn't anything he could do for me that my body couldn't do better. I had to suffer through this time until my body expelled the bullets. Since they weren't silver, or laced with it, they weren't going to kill me. Chester was a shit shot, and I was thankful he'd been so close to me when he'd pulled the trigger. Crazy, yeah, but it meant he didn't get lucky and put a bullet in my brain. *That* wasn't survivable.

I looked up at Harlan as I took as deep breaths as I

could. I set a hand over my chest, trying to ease the pain. "Thanks," I told him.

He nodded and remained silent, yet he was watchful. Like Rachel was.

He was concerned for me. Even though he knew I'd be fine, he looked worried.

"You saved my mate," I said.

Harlan nodded.

"Thank you. Where's Chester?"

"Dead."

"I called Holt, the Sheriff, to deal with it," Cord said. "He's a shifter," he explained. "He'll make sure it looks like a car accident killed Chester."

"Why were you here?" I asked Harlan. Most of my anger from earlier had dissipated the moment he'd returned with my mate intact. Whatever he'd done in the past, he'd just protected the most precious thing to me in this world. I owed him for that.

He scratched his stubbled chin. "I came because I need to explain what happened with your mom, just... just so you know."

"You should listen, Nash," Cord said.

Fuck. "I'm sorry. I owe you more than an apology. I owe you a chance to explain."

Rachel came back and knelt beside the chair,

although she wasn't sure where to set the towel. I took it from her and pressed it against the worst wound.

"Sit, please," Cord told Harlan, holding his arm out and pointing to another chair.

Harlan dropped into it as if the weight of the world pushed him down.

I braced myself for his story.

"Noble and I became scent matches when he turned fifteen," he said. "We knew it, and found out one full moon run. I was older by years. I thought I didn't have one."

I glanced at Cord, who hadn't found his scent match until he was over thirty.

A bullet came to the surface, and I hissed as my body rejected it.

Rachel gasped and took it, stared at it and then up at me. I stroked her hair, not caring that I was streaking it with blood.

"I'm okay," I told her.

She smiled and a tear slid down her cheek. Somehow that bullet appearing eased her, and she took my hand in hers and turned to face Harlan. To listen to his story.

I didn't have a choice but to wait for the rest of the bullets to emerge. And listen.

Harlan sensed I was ready to hear more, so he continued. "We didn't go to school together, or live nearby on pack land. Our families weren't close. The only thing we had in common was the scent match. After we discovered it, I didn't see him for years. Not until we went to the pack games."

The games were a week of organized outdoor events meant to bring packs together from all over the country, for the purpose of shifters finding their true mates. Some even from Canada. They happened every July, and were hosted by different packs. I'd been to a few.

Harlan ran a hand over his face. I knew now what I was going to look like in thirty-some years, but I had to hope the outdoors wouldn't age me as quickly.

"By then, I was seeing the signs of moon madness," he added. "Aggression. The desire to stay in wolf form for longer and longer periods. Difficulty changing back to human form. I figured if I didn't find my mate that summer, I could succumb to the madness and they'd have to put me down. But Fate was on my side. Or at least, I thought so, because I picked up Cathryn's scent. I found Noble, who was also there. The attraction was powerful. We all felt the pull."

He sighed and looked out a window, but was seeing into the past, not the forest.

"That first day of finding my mate. Fuck, I remember how intense and sweet it was. She was mine."

"And Noble?" Cord asked.

Harlan looked at him. "He agreed. It was potent. Good. Cathryn and Noble were close in age. They bonded quickly, not that I didn't. But my wolf rode me hard. Pushed me to claim her. She was receptive. Open to the claiming."

"What's the claiming?" Rachel asked.

I winced, hating that we'd kept her in the dark about our kind.

"When a male wolf, or two wolves in our species' case, find their true mate, they bite her to permanently embed their scent and mark her as theirs." Cord's gaze on Rachel heated. "You're our true mate. That's how we knew we wanted you so quickly, and then realized we were scent matches and meant to share you."

"Oh." Rachel's eyes were wide. Her face flushed a pretty shade of pink.

I knew the feelings Harlan spoke of. The need for Rachel, the craving to claim her. Cord had been forced to stop me the other night, the desperation to mark her had been so powerful. I'd do anything to get my scent in her, and I wasn't moon mad.

"I'm sorry, go on," Rachel said to Harlan.

"We couldn't wait to claim—" Harlan began.

I grunted and arched my back as another bullet came to the surface and was expelled. Waving my hand, I got him to continue.

"The moon was full. There were bonfires, and everything was festive. We didn't wait a single night to claim Cathryn. We went to my place..." Harlan broke off like he didn't want to go on.

My stomach churned. "What happened?"

"I don't know. One minute, we were pleasuring our she-wolf, the next, I'd turned savage trying to claim her. To this day, I don't remember those minutes that passed between me sinking my teeth into her flesh—and finding myself in wolf form with the two of them bloodied and cornered in my room."

"Moon madness can come on in spurts in the beginning," Cord said. He glanced at Rachel to explain. "It's what happens if a dominant wolf meets his true mate but doesn't claim her—or, in cases of alpha wolves, if he doesn't find his true mate by his mid-thirties. His wolf goes mad, and he turns feral. It's where the human lore about werewolves originates."

Rachel's eyes grew even larger. "Oh."

I squeezed her hand to reassure her. "You're safe. We'd never let anything like that happen to you."

"I figured I'd gone moon mad, and ran as far away from civilization as I could. But then," Harlan's throat worked and he blinked rapidly, "then I recovered. I guess claiming Cathryn cured me. Only it was too late. I'd hurt her and Noble—badly. They were afraid. When the alpha tried to bring me back to the pack, they objected, strongly. They refused to believe I was safe, and left the pack."

I stared at Harlan, shaken to my core by his story. It was almost worse to hear he'd been innocent, betrayed by biology, than to believe he was guilty. Because the difference between the two of us had just lessened. My wolf had been overly aggressive with Rachel, growing increasingly more frantic as the days went by without my marking her. My fear of harming Rachel was legitimate.

As if Cord read my mind, he said, "You've shown no signs of moon madness, Nash. Just the strong desire to claim your true mate, same as I feel."

I gave him a bleak stare. "My aggression..." I choked.

"You'll keep it in check. We can handle it."

"The sooner you two claim your mate, the better," Harlan advised.

Nash and I both shot him an irritated look.

"Rachel just found out what we are a half hour ago," Cord said drily. "We'll give her all the time she needs."

"I don't need time," Rachel spoke quietly beside me.

My hand tightened in hers. "Wolves mate for life," I warned. "This is a lifetime commitment. It's more than a marriage certificate. And we know you're still trying to find yourself."

"You both need to claim me, or you could die. There's nothing to consider," she said fiercely, showing that same backbone I'd seen when she stood up to her father. "Besides... I think I have found myself. It's here in West Springs. It's being with you two."

My wolf circled with joy, but I still had a sense of dread. What if I hurt her like Harlan had hurt my mother? I turned my attention back to him. "So what happened in Montana?" I needed to know the entire story.

"After a year had passed and they still hadn't returned to West Springs, I decided to go visit the Wolf Ranch pack, and talk to Cathryn's parents. I didn't know where Noble and Cathryn had gone, but I wanted to try to put my family back together," Harlan said. He scrubbed a hand across his face. "I should have contacted their alpha first to ask permission, but of course, I was afraid it wouldn't be given. No one here trusted me, it made sense no one there would believe my story, either. I didn't know my showing up would spook them so badly. When I pulled up at Cathryn's parents' house, Cathryn and Noble bolted for their car. I followed. I just wanted a chance to talk to them. To explain how devastated I was, and that I would never harm them again. But they were scared of me." He rubbed his mouth, and his hand shook as he lowered it.

"I shouldn't have followed. I should have stayed to talk to your grandparents, instead. But my wolf needed to be with both of them so badly, I chased after them. It was winter, and the roads were icy. A boulder had rolled down the incline and lay in the middle of the road. Noble swerved to miss it, and skidded off the edge."

Harlan's eyes turned red and he blinked rapidly. "I didn't mean to kill them, but I was responsible. I took your parents from you, son, and not a day goes by I'm not sorry for that."

I blinked back tears of my own. "Fuck." That's all there was to say about it. All I could think of, anyway.

"It's true," Cord said.

I shifted in my chair to get more comfortable. I figured there was one more bullet in me. The other two were through-and-throughs, and I just had to wait for the wounds to heal up. I pressed a hand on my gut and felt the hard metal.

Rachel came up on her knees and looked down at the wound. "I'm all right, beautiful," I murmured.

"I talked to Gibson," Cord said. "Got the old alpha's records."

Harlan stared at him, wide-eyed.

Cord set his hand on the older man's shoulder. "Your story matches."

"You went to the alpha?" Harlan asked.

Cord nodded. "I wanted the truth. Facts are better than gossip."

I couldn't help but laugh, then grimace. "The doctor does like proof."

Something shifted in Harlan. A wariness that had been about him since I met him—fuck, was it only a few hours earlier?—left him. A smile turned up the corners of his mouth.

"No one's ever believed me. Noble and Cathryn..." He pulled a bandana from the back pocket of his jeans, and wiped at his eyes.

"They didn't give you the chance to explain," Rachel said, getting to her feet and taking Harlan's hand.

He shook his head.

"Neither did anyone in the pack?" she asked.

"Jack West knew the truth, but it didn't matter."

"You banished yourself," I added.

Pushing off the arms of the chair, I stood. Rachel came over to me and propped me up. I didn't need her help but I wasn't going to let her know that. Her concern and caring filled a well inside me I hadn't known was empty.

"Yes. I didn't mean to scare my mates. I didn't mean to push them to hide from me. To hide *you* from me."

Fuck. He'd done nothing wrong, and hadn't even known he'd had a child. For almost thirty years, he'd isolated himself, afraid of what was inside of him.

He'd missed out on so much. He'd fled.

So had I.

"Fuck," I breathed.

"What? Are you hurt?" Rachel asked, running her hands over me. That sure as hell felt good, even as I had a bullet working its way out of my body and I had an epiphany about how much of a dumbass I'd been.

"I'm fine. I realized that I was about to do the same thing."

Rachel frowned. "What do you mean?"

I cupped her face. "I'm rough with you. Wild. I thought... I thought I was tainted." I tipped my head toward Harlan. "Like father, like son."

She narrowed her eyes as she looked up at me. "I hope so. Your father is brave and protective and courageous and kind." She went up on her tiptoes and whispered in my ear. "I told you, I like it rough."

I couldn't help but smile. Yeah, my mate was a little she-wolf in the sack.

I released my hold on Rachel and went to my father. Met his gaze that was identical to mine.

"I'm sorry I didn't give you a chance earlier."

He looked away and waved me off.

"Thank you for saving our mate. I am forever grateful."

Harlan cleared his throat. "That's what family does. Takes care of each other."

Cord shook Harlan's hand as I continued to look at the man I'd never expected to be alive. To look like me. To act like the man I hoped to emulate.

There wasn't anything else I could do but hug him.

For a second, he stood stock still, then his hands moved around me and he hugged me back.

He stepped back first. "I think you've got one more job to do. That mate of yours, lock her down. Claim her. *Carefully.*"

I ran a hand over the back of my neck and looked to Cord.

"Listen to your elders," Cord said.

We both turned and faced Rachel.

She bit her lip. "You said this claiming thing... it means forever for shifters?"

We nodded in unison.

"Good."

22

RACHEL

"ARE YOU SURE?" Cord asked, his large hands settling on my waist.

The three of us were in Cord's bedroom. Harlan had left—but agreed to return soon—and Nash had showered to clean off the blood. He was up and moving around without a problem now. His wounds looked weeks old, not hours. Only a bit of puckered pink flesh remained.

It was a lot to take in, but honestly, no more than believing two incredibly hot guys wanted to share me.

The wolf part just felt like the missing piece of the puzzle. Now it all made sense.

I couldn't complain or freak about my guys being part wolves because... well, it had saved Nash's life. If Nash was a mere human, he'd be dead.

It was insane to think that these two hot cowboys were biologically wired to be with me. To share me. We were destined for each other. That was why I'd landed in West Springs. That was why they felt so right to me. That was why they said 'fates' all the time instead of swearing. It had been fate that brought us together.

"I'm sure," I murmured. That moment when Chester shot Nash had been the worst of my life. Being wrenched by Chester from the two men I'd already come to love had been like having a limb chopped off. Thinking he was dead—

"I'm not," Nash said.

Nash had almost walked away from our threesome for fear he'd hurt me like Harlan had hurt his mom. I wasn't about to let that happen.

"You won't hurt me." I was sure of it. After all we'd been through, I was more sure than ever. Any doubt I had was gone now.

He swallowed, eyed me with that determined, yet

haunted, gaze. "You're human, Rach. If I fuck up, there's no instant healing. No do-overs."

"You won't hurt me," I repeated. I took his face in my hands and made my voice firm. "How you touch me isn't violent. Isn't dangerous for me. I love it, how you feel about me. How you show it when you touch me."

"Didn't Harlan reassure you? You're not feral. You're not moon mad. You're not dangerous," Cord told Nash. "I agree with Rach. You touch her in your own way. I see how she is aroused by it. Needs it."

Nash thought for another moment, then nodded.

"Now, what does this claiming involve?" I asked.

Nash's eyes changed to silvery-blue. Cord's turned yellow.

I wasn't afraid. I couldn't wait to see their wolves. Wolves! How insane was that?

"Usually the bite would happen during or right after orgasm. But I was thinking it might be better if Nash marks you before he's in the throes of it. When his passion-level is dialed down. Just to be safe," Cord said.

A hint of pain while coming? My pussy clenched at the idea. I wasn't thrilled about being bitten instead of a playful nip, but I trusted them. They needed this, and I'd give them anything.

Nash had protected me from Chester with his body. I'd thought he'd died for me. I could have an extra intense orgasm with a little wolf kink thrown in.

Nash visibly relaxed at Cord's suggestion. "I like that idea."

"You were ready to mark her that first day at the barbecue, just from a kiss. You think you could just give her a nip and get it done with? That should calm your wolf's strong urge to claim, and then you can focus on making it good for her," Cord added.

A hint of a smile curved Nash's lips. It was the first time I'd seen him smile all day, and it set off flutters in my chest. "Yeah. I know exactly how this should go." He stepped up behind me so I was sandwiched between the two men. He tugged my shirt off over my head. Cord unbuttoned my jeans. In a matter of seconds, they had stripped off my clothes. I started to work the buttons on Cord's shirt, but I didn't have time to finish, because Nash picked me up and deposited me on my back in the center of the bed.

"Spread those legs wide for me, beautiful," he said, taking in every inch of me. "I know just where I want to mark you."

More flutters.

I parted my thighs as he stripped out of his clothes and climbed onto the bed. He knelt below me and scooped his hands under my knees to push them up and open.

Oh my.

"Have you ever seen such a beautiful pussy, Cord?" Nash asked.

"Never in my life." Cord climbed up behind me and slid his legs around me, propping my back and shoulders up against his chest so he could toy with my nipples. "Our mate is as perfect as they come."

"Even though I'm not a... she-wolf?" I asked, tipping my head to glance up at Cord. I wasn't sure if the word was right, but he nodded.

"Perfect," Nash said firmly. "I wouldn't want you any other way." He distracted me from any other questions I might have asked by settling between my thighs and licking into me.

I shivered, my hips bucking to meet his mouth. My nipples pebbled up under Cord's gentle pinching and tweaking.

Whoever thought being with two men was wrong had never felt like this.

Nash took his time, flicking the tip of his tongue over my clit until it swelled and throbbed, then circling it. He sucked one of my labia into his mouth, then penetrated me with his tongue. "You taste so fucking sweet. I could eat you out all day. Keep dripping for me, beautiful, and I'll lick it all up."

I moaned, closing my eyes and letting the sensations wash over me. The sense of surrender was complete—all I had to do was let go and let my wolf-mates take care of me.

Nash pushed my knees up higher toward my shoulders to roll my pelvis up off the bed, and then he licked me from anus to clit. I squealed at the sensations, my inner thighs quivering, my breath coming in short pants. He penetrated me with his tongue again, a slow in and out that was not nearly enough, and made me crazy with need.

When he lifted his head, his lips were glossy with my juices, and his eyes wolf-bright. "I was thinking right here." He traced a circle on my inner thigh as his gaze met Cord's above my head. "Then I can see my mark every time my mouth is on her sweet pussy."

"Are you ready, Rachel?" Cord asked. "Nash will be gentle." I suspected Cord was saying the words as much as a reminder to Nash as they were a comfort to me.

"Go ahead." My voice sounded husky, as if the idea of being bitten by a wolf was as sexy as having his cock inside of me. It wasn't like he could fuck me and bite my inner thigh at the same time. He had to do it now.

Nash held Cord's gaze a moment longer, and I suspected there was some unspoken agreement between them. I didn't know what it was, but I trusted them. I was between them. Theirs, in all things.

Nash lowered his head and licked the place he'd been circling with his fingertip. I buried my fingers in his hair to show him I was with him. He brought his thumb to my clit and rubbed it at the same time as he struck—a swift penetration of his teeth into the soft flesh of my thigh muscle.

I jerked in surprise. It hurt, but I was distracted from the pain by the sight of release rippling through Nash's body. Even though the previous pleasure had been all for me, his hips bucked and his cock jutted out ramrod straight beneath him, cum spewing from the tip. I orgasmed, too, reaching down to use my fingers between my legs.

Nash released his teeth from my thigh and licked the wound, then joined his fingers with mine to help me ride out my finish. I cried out in satisfaction.

"Fates, that was beautiful." Cord's hot breath feathered across my ear. "Are you okay, Rachel?"

"Yes, I'm okay." I arched my breasts for more of his touch. "I'm more than okay. Married and marked."

A growl escaped Nash. In a flash, he had me flipped over to my hands and knees above Cord.

"Climb onto your mate, beautiful," Nash guided me.

He wanted me to fuck Cord now.

I was all for that. The one orgasm wasn't enough. Not even close.

Nash's lips were on my shoulder. His hands stroked down my back. I lifted my hips up over Cord's generous erection and positioned myself, rubbing the head of his cock over my entrance.

"You want him to wear a condom, or is bareback okay from now on?" Nash asked.

Obviously, I'd never gone bare with anyone before since Nash and Cord were the only guys I'd slept with. The idea of nothing between us... my pussy clenched in eagerness.

"It's okay. I'm on the pill," I said, then covered my mouth with my fingers for a second. "I'm sorry." God, I didn't think, remembering that Cord couldn't get me pregnant.

"Shit," Nash muttered.

"I'm clean," Cord said. "I'd never put you in danger even if shifters could get STDs."

"I'm clean, too," I said, meeting Cord's dark eyes. "Recent virgin and all that."

"Beautiful, it's fine. It bothered me before, but after all we've been through, we have each other. If you want pups... babies, we'll give them to you. Nash won't mind."

Nash chuckled behind me. "My pleasure."

Cord smiled. "We'll adopt. Whatever."

"You're not less," I whispered, and leaned down to kiss him.

"I know," he said when I lifted my head. "Everything's good. And I'm glad you're on the pill. We'll get that baby in you—when you're ready."

I nodded, relieved I hadn't goofed. Glad that Cord knew he wasn't 'less.' Nothing could make me see him that way. I wanted to prove it to him, so I lowered myself over him, feeding in his length inch by delicious inch. I wanted him, and he couldn't deny it now.

Cord groaned with pleasure as I settled onto his lap, his dick buried deep.

I held still, adjusting to his size. Setting my hands on his chest, I began to move, lifting and lowering and circling my hips, following the pleasure.

"Cord, you feel so good," I said.

His hands gripped my hips. His fingers squeezed as he began to help, thrusting up into me.

"Come here, beautiful." Cord cupped the back of my neck and pulled me down for a kiss. Our tongues tangled as he fucked up into me.

A hand stroked down the length of my spine. Nash.

"Time to take both of us," he murmured.

I wasn't sure when he'd grabbed the lube, but the cold liquid dribbled down over my ass. Nash's finger gently circled my back entrance, just like last time. But now, it wasn't going to be his thumb in me as my pussy was filled. It was going to be his dick.

I was going to be fucked by both my men.

I gasped when Nash carefully worked a finger into me.

Cord groaned, and thrust harder. The combination of both men in me, touching me, had me close to coming again.

I had no idea how long Nash played for, but he'd worked lube into me and stretched me open as Cord kissed and fucked me. Nash's fingers moved away, and I felt him lean over me.

"Time to take both your mates," he breathed, and I felt his hardness there. A gentle press. Constant.

Cord stilled beneath me, buried deep.

I tried to breathe as Nash pushed, and carefully opened me up.

Just like my heart, my body could give no resistance to an insistent male. The flared crown of his cock popped inside me.

I lifted my head and moaned.

So full.

God, it was intense.

"Good girl," Cord said. He whispered to me, dark and dirty promises, as Nash slid further and further into me.

Cord stroked my hair, kissed me. Crooned.

Then Nash stilled. "Fuck, beautiful. You're perfect. Taking both your males. I'm going to come, and we're not even moving."

"It's time," Cord practically growled. The heat radiating from his body made me start to sweat. He was tense. Desperate.

"Please," I begged, needing more. Needing something.

Nash pulled back as Cord thrust deep.

"Oh!" I cried.

Nash pressed into me as Cord lifted my hips, slipping almost all the way from my pussy.

They went on like that, alternating movements as I could do nothing but cling to Cord. Moan. Gasp. Cry out from the intense pleasure.

I had no idea it could be like this, it was overwhelming.

"I can't... I'm going to... I need—"

"It's time, beautiful," Cord said.

I blinked and saw him eye my neck. He tugged on my hips and thrust deep as he lifted his head and bit my shoulder.

I tossed my head back and came. The hint of pain mingled with Nash deep in my ass and Cord's dick pulsing and filling me with his cum in my pussy made the pleasure so intense, I screamed. I writhed, yet I couldn't move, caught between my men.

Cord lifted his head and licked the spot he'd bitten, but I couldn't focus on that. Couldn't focus on anything but the orgasm. How they made me feel. How it didn't stop. Wouldn't.

I finally collapsed onto Cord, all loose limbs and melted bones. Nash carefully pulled out and left the bed. Cord slipped from me and settled me into his arms. I might have dozed, because I felt a warm washcloth cleaning me up.

Next, I was snuggled between them, warm, comforted. Protected. Cherished.

"Ours," Nash growled, nipping at my shoulder playfully.

I giggled.

"Yours," I agreed, ready for anything with these two. I didn't know what my future was going to hold, but I knew it had Cord and Nash in it.

23

ORD

TWO WEEKS HAD PASSED and they had been the best weeks of my life.

I hadn't realized how I'd focused my attention so much on helping others and my genetic studies that I'd missed that there was a world out there. Even in a small town like West Springs, I'd missed so much. Being focused on not having a scent match, I'd felt sorry for myself. I'd thought that the fact that I couldn't have kids made me worthless.

I didn't feel it now. Yes, I'd found my scent match, but even that couldn't fix broken biology. I still couldn't give Rachel kids, but it didn't bother me any longer. I didn't have to give them to Rachel. All I had to give her was myself.

Which I did, wholeheartedly. And which she wanted.

The second Nash scented Rachel, he'd relocated to West Springs. Wherever she was, he was. We'd gone together to the Wolf Ranch pack and brought some of his things back so he could settle here, passing the work of his construction company over to his partner, Rand. We'd seen where he'd lived, met his friends and pack mates. Gone to his grandparents' graves.

He wasn't looking at the past any longer, but the future.

So was I.

We had Rachel.

We also had Harlan.

"Honey, I can't believe what Chester put you through." Rachel's dad couldn't let it go. While Rachel had walked away from Chester at their engagement party, her parents had continued to believe he was the man for their daughter.

Until she called and told them what Chester had done—or a sanitized version that didn't involve Nash getting shot five times in the chest.

After that, it had taken a week for her parents to

come to terms with the danger their daughter had been in, and that they'd trusted a crazy asshole instead of their own child. They'd put a perceived happiness over the truth.

Then they'd bought plane tickets and flown to Wyoming.

They were here. With us. Now.

It was hard not to go to Rachel and pull her onto my lap. Kiss her. Show her how much she meant to me, even while her father worked through it all. Chester's betrayal, Rachel's 'finding herself' in Montana, her marriage to Nash.

For them, I needed to play the part of friend, not mate, which was fine. I sat across the room while Rachel and Nash sat next to her parents.

"It's fine, Dad," Rachel said, placating him. Again.

We were at Gibson's for another barbecue. This time, the group was smaller. Gibson, Ben, and Shelby, since it was their house. Marne, Shelby's mom. The three of us. Rachel's parents, and Harlan.

I had come with Rachel again, but with Nash, instead of fighting him over the baked beans. We had a common goal: our mate.

We were all shifters except for Rachel and her parents. We not only had to keep that a secret, but also that we mated in pairs.

"He shot at your husband!" Rachel's father ran a hand through his thinning salt and pepper hair. Her mother sat next to him on the couch in the great room, patting his thigh. They looked out of place in the cabin, like they'd gone to play golf at their country club but somehow ended up in Wyoming instead. They were still distraught over what had happened, and trying to process it all. As shifters, we didn't panic about being shot, so we'd all come to terms with what happened fairly quickly.

I remembered her father's call when he'd first learned of Rachel's marriage to Nash. How insulting he'd been. How he'd believed every lie Chester had dished out.

Oh, how he'd changed his tune.

The man was around sixty, and wore khakis and a plaid button-up. The kind golfers wore in the winter, not the flannel lumberjack variety. Rachel's mother wore a dress and heels, more appropriate for a dinner party than a rural Wyoming barbecue, but they were who they were.

They loved Rachel, and that was all I cared about.

"He did, Dad," Rachel said, taking a sip of her wine. "It's over now."

The man took a deep breath as if trying to calm himself. "He kidnapped you and drove into a ditch. He was killed!" He grabbed Rachel's hand in his. "God, I don't know how you survived."

Rachel's mom wiped her eyes with a handkerchief.

"I had just found her. No way would she be taken from me," Nash told him.

Rachel's mom nodded and set her hand over her heart. Nash had won them over with his quick grin and kind heart. It was also the way he obviously loved Rachel that had worked the most.

Nash was sitting beside Rachel and he pulled her back into his hold, her back resting against his chest. He kissed her hair. Which was what I wanted to do.

"I had him checked out," her dad added, frowning. "Huge gambling debts. He was about to be kicked out of the club."

"We're so sorry, love," her mom said. "We pushed you so much. You coming here... it was like fate or something."

Rachel smiled and gave Nash a quick glance. Definitely fate.

"I know, Mom," she said. "We've talked about this all week since you arrived. I'm fine. I'm happy. I love Nash."

She glanced my way, met my gaze. I knew she silently added that she loved me too.

"Love at first sight," her mom whispered, then started crying again.

Rachel sighed and looked to Nash, who kissed her on the lips this time.

"We have my father to thank," Nash said.

Everyone looked at Harlan, who was standing by the kitchen counter where the appetizers were laid out.

He wasn't used to crowds, although this wasn't even that. Being alone for so long, he was uncomfortable around people. We'd visited him several times since the incident, slowly getting to know him. Gibson had announced to the pack what had happened thirty years ago, dispelling any rumors, and ensuring everyone knew Harlan was welcome within the pack.

Rachel had shared details of what had happened with her parents, embellishing some parts and outright lying about others. She couldn't share that Harlan had shifted to wolf form and ripped Chester's throat out. She couldn't share that Nash had actually been shot and then quickly healed on his own. She couldn't share that we were a triad.

But what we had offered them was enough to bring them around. That the sheriff had been involved. That Chester had acted alone, and because of bad choices he made in California.

"We're family now," Rachel said. She looked to Harlan, then to her parents. "All of us."

Her father nodded. "We just want you happy, honey."

"I know," Rachel murmured. "Just so you know, I could have been a senator."

Her father's eyes widened as if the idea had never occurred to him. Then he smiled. "Yes, you could have. Still can."

Nash raised his hand. "Whatever my wife wants," he began. "But she's going to make a mighty fine teacher. I think that's a better way to serve the community."

I couldn't agree more.

Shelby came down the stairs with Marne, and introductions were made to Rachel's parents. I didn't miss how Harlan saw Marne, and couldn't look away.

I stood and went around the seating area to join him. "Want me to get her over here?"

Harlan blinked and looked at me. His cheeks flushed, and he shifted his gaze to the cheese and crackers.

"I don't think that's a good idea," he murmured.

After three decades, it was going to take a while for him to assimilate back into pack life. And a pretty woman like Marne? Maybe she was just the thing he needed.

"The alpha has announced your return," I told him. "You should be proud of what you did, saving Rachel. The entire pack is."

We watched as Shelby laughed at something Rachel's mom said.

Ben came in from the deck, the scent of grilled meat following him. "The burgers are almost done."

Shelby stood and went over to him. Marne followed.

"Marne, this is—" I began to make introductions, but she smiled brightly at Harlan.

"The rescuer. It's so nice to meet you," Marne said, taking Harlan's hand and holding it between hers. "I heard what you did," she whispered. "We'll do anything for our children, won't we?" She glanced at Shelby, then back at Harlan.

His face was ruddy with embarrassment, but a smile turned his lips up. "Yes, ma'am."

"I'd like a glass of wine and maybe a chat. Let these young folk do their thing."

Somehow, she took hold of his elbow and steered the smitten shifter away.

Shelby snorted. "I'd been hoping Mom would find someone. Looks like she might have."

"He needs some coaxing," I added. I knew Harlan had been matched to Cathryn, and I knew Marne had had a mate who'd left her. Both had been alone for a long time. Shifters got together even without being fated mates, so maybe this was a second chance for both of them.

Shelby set her hand on my back. "Oh, if a female sets her sights on a man, watch out."

I arched a brow, wondering if Rachel was using her wiles on me and Nash. Did I care? Hell, no.

We turned to the group. Gibson brought in a platter of burgers, steam rising off them. Ben called everyone to the counter to serve themselves buffet style.

Nash stood and tugged Rachel with him, keeping her close.

Rachel's parents watched, and couldn't miss the love their daughter had for her husband.

Was I jealous? Definitely. I had known going in what it would be like, that I couldn't outwardly share my affection for my mate with humans. As long as she was in my bed later, I knew everything was going to be fine.

Nash went to grab a plate, pointing out things to Rachel's parents as Rachel came up to me.

"You're mine," she whispered.

I was instantly hard. "I know," I replied.

"Later, I'm going to show you how much."

I growled low.

Nash turned to glance at me, then grinned, obviously hearing the low sound.

"Promise?" I murmured.

Rachel nodded and left me to go and fix herself a plate.

I watched the group. This mix of shifters and humans. Rachel's parents, who had no clue about the depth of the secrets that surrounded them. There was no doubt about the love they had for their daughter. They would slowly learn to change their perceptions of Rachel, their expectations. If what her father said was true and they only wanted her happy, then we were in agreement.

That was my goal in life now. To make Rachel happy.

Nash would agree.

Gibson and Ben had Shelby, and it was obvious she was content in their match.

And Harlan and Marne, who had picked up plates to fill? Time would tell.

I didn't question any longer. I knew. I had all the facts.

I had a scent match. A mate. The perfect match.

Ready for more Two Marks? Read Enticed now!

NOTE FROM VANESSA & RENEE

Guess what? We've got some bonus content for you with Rachel, Cord and Nash. Yup, there's more!

Click here to read!

WANT FREE RENEE ROSE BOOKS?

In addition to the free stories, you will also get special pricing, exclusive previews and news of new releases.

GET A FREE VANESSA VALE BOOK!

Join my mailing list to be the first to know of new releases, free books, special prices and other author giveaways.

http://freeromanceread.com

More Mafia Romance

Her Russian Master

Contemporary

Daddy Rules Series

Fire Daddy

Hollywood Daddy

Stepbrother Daddy

Master Me Series

Her Royal Master

Her Russian Master

Her Marine Master

Yes, Doctor

Double Doms Series

Theirs to Punish

Theirs to Protect

Holiday Feel-Good

Scoring with Santa

Saved

Wolf Ridge High Series

Alpha Bully

Alpha Knight

Bad Boy Alphas Series

Alpha's Temptation

Alpha's Danger

Alpha's Prize

Alpha's Challenge

Alpha's Obsession

Alpha's Desire

Alpha's War

Alpha's Mission

Alpha's Bane

Alpha's Secret

Alpha's Prey

Alpha's Sun

Shifter Ops

Alpha's Moon

Alpha's Vow

Alpha's Revenge

His Human Possession

Zandian Brides

Night of the Zandians

Bought by the Zandians

Mastered by the Zandians

Zandian Lights

Kept by the Zandian

Claimed by the Zandian

Stolen by the Zandian

Other Sci-Fi

The Hand of Vengeance

Her Alien Masters

Regency

The Darlington Incident

Humbled

The Reddington Scandal

The Westerfield Affair

Pleasing the Colonel

Western

ABOUT RENEE ROSE

USA TODAY BESTSELLING AUTHOR RENEE ROSE loves a dominant, dirty-talking alpha hero! She's sold over a million copies of steamy romance with varying levels of kink. Her books have been featured in USA Today's *Happily Ever After* and *Popsugar*. Named Eroticon USA's Next Top Erotic Author in 2013, she has also won *Spunky and Sassy's* Favorite Sci-Fi and Anthology author, *The Romance Reviews* Best Historical Romance, and *has* hit the *USA Today* list eight times with her Bad Boy Alpha and Wolf Ranch series, as well as various anthologies.

Please follow her on Tiktok

Renee loves to connect with readers!
www.reneeroseromance.com
reneeroseauthor@gmail.com

ABOUT VANESSA VALE

Vanessa Vale is the *USA Today* bestselling author of sexy romance novels, including her popular Bridgewater historical series and hot contemporary romances. With over one million books sold, Vanessa writes about unapologetic bad boys who don't just fall in love, they fall hard. Her books are available worldwide in multiple languages in e-book, print, audio and even as an online game. When she's not writing, Vanessa savors the insanity of raising two boys and figuring out how many meals she can make with a pressure cooker. While she's not as skilled at social media as her kids, she loves to interact with readers.

BookBub

Instagram

Made in United States
North Haven, CT
05 November 2021

10870918R00164

I CRAVE HER SCENT. I CAN'T STAY AWAY.

Nothing can keep me from claiming the new waitress at
diner. Except for her other mate, the scent match I didr
know existed. He's a stranger to me and our pack, but n
we must work together.

TWO MATES FOR OUR FEMALE.

Our mate is human, untouched. She doesn't know about
kind. We must convince her to accept not one, but two mc
Two cowboys in her bed. Two dominant wolves to protect
And my scent match's wolf is turning feral with need.

WE TOUCH OUR MATE. WE CAN'T GET ENOUGH.

We need to claim her and mark her as ours before his w
goes mad. She's a virgin, so we have to be careful—shift
can be rough. And we're not the only ones who want
her—she's being hunted by another male. But I will prote
her if it's the last thing I do. Even if it means keeping h
from her other mate.

VANESSAVALEAUTHOR.COM

RENEEROSEROMANCE.COM

ISBN 9798754456372

9000

9 798754 456372